Face of Murder

BOOKS BY BLAKE PIERCE

THE AU PAIR SERIES

ALMOST GONE (Book#1)

ALMOST LOST (Book #2)

ALMOST DEAD (Book #3)

ZOE PRIME MYSTERY SERIES

FACE OF DEATH (Book#1)

FACE OF MURDER (Book #2)

FACE OF FEAR (Book #3)

A JESSIE HUNT PSYCHOLOGICAL SUSPENSE SERIES

THE PERFECT WIFE (Book #1)

THE PERFECT BLOCK (Book #2)

THE PERFECT HOUSE (Book #3)

THE PERFECT SMILE (Book #4)

THE PERFECT LIE (Book #5)

THE PERFECT LOOK (Book #6)

CHLOE FINE PSYCHOLOGICAL SUSPENSE SERIES

NEXT DOOR (Book #1)

A NEIGHBOR'S LIE (Book #2)

CUL DE SAC (Book #3)

SILENT NEIGHBOR (Book #4)

HOMECOMING (Book #5)

TINTED WINDOWS (Book #6)

KATE WISE MYSTERY SERIES

IF SHE KNEW (Book #1)

IF SHE SAW (Book #2)
IF SHE RAN (Book #3)
IF SHE HID (Book #4)
IF SHE FLED (Book #5)
IF SHE FEARED (Book #6)
IF SHE HEARD (Book #7)

THE MAKING OF RILEY PAIGE SERIES

WATCHING (Book #1)
WAITING (Book #2)
LURING (Book #3)
TAKING (Book #4)
STALKING (Book #5)

RILEY PAIGE MYSTERY SERIES

ONCE GONE (Book #1)
ONCE TAKEN (Book #2)
ONCE CRAVED (Book #3)
ONCE LURED (Book #4)
ONCE HUNTED (Book #5)
ONCE PINED (Book #6)
ONCE FORSAKEN (Book #7)
ONCE COLD (Book #8)
ONCE STALKED (Book #9)
ONCE LOST (Book #10)
ONCE BURIED (Book #11)
ONCE BOUND (Book #12)
ONCE TRAPPED (Book #13)
ONCE DORMANT (Book #14)
ONCE SHUNNED (Book #15)
ONCE MISSED (Book #16)
ONCE CHOSEN (Book #17)

MACKENZIE WHITE MYSTERY SERIES

BEFORE HE KILLS (Book #1)

BEFORE HE SEES (Book #2)
BEFORE HE COVETS (Book #3)
BEFORE HE TAKES (Book #4)
BEFORE HE NEEDS (Book #5)
BEFORE HE FEELS (Book #6)
BEFORE HE SINS (Book #7)
BEFORE HE HUNTS (Book #8)
BEFORE HE PREYS (Book #9)
BEFORE HE LONGS (Book #10)
BEFORE HE LAPSES (Book #11)
BEFORE HE ENVIES (Book #12)
BEFORE HE STALKS (Book #13)
BEFORE HE HARMS (Book #14)

AVERY BLACK MYSTERY SERIES

CAUSE TO KILL (Book #1)
CAUSE TO RUN (Book #2)
CAUSE TO HIDE (Book #3)
CAUSE TO FEAR (Book #4)
CAUSE TO SAVE (Book #5)
CAUSE TO DREAD (Book #6)

KERI LOCKE MYSTERY SERIES

A TRACE OF DEATH (Book #1)
A TRACE OF MUDER (Book #2)
A TRACE OF VICE (Book #3)
A TRACE OF CRIME (Book #4)
A TRACE OF HOPE (Book #5)

Face of Murder

(A Zoe Prime Mystery—Book 2)

Blake Pierce

Blake Pierce

Blake Pierce is the USA Today bestselling author of the RILEY PAGE mystery series, which includes sixteen books (and counting). Blake Pierce is also the author of the MACKENZIE WHITE mystery series, comprising thirteen books (and counting); of the AVERY BLACK mystery series, comprising six books; of the KERI LOCKE mystery series, comprising five books; of the MAKING OF RILEY PAIGE mystery series, comprising five books (and counting); of the KATE WISE mystery series, comprising six books (and counting); of the CHLOE FINE psychological suspense mystery, comprising five books (and counting); of the JESSE HUNT psychological suspense thriller series, comprising five books (and counting); of the AU PAIR psychological suspense thriller series, comprising two books (and counting); and of the ZOE PRIME mystery series, comprising two books (and counting).

ONCE GONE (a Riley Paige Mystery—Book #1), BEFORE HE KILLS (A Mackenzie White Mystery—Book 1), CAUSE TO KILL (An Avery Black Mystery—Book 1), A TRACE OF DEATH (A Keri Locke Mystery—Book 1), and WATCHING (The Making of Riley Paige—Book 1) are each available as a free download on Amazon!

An avid reader and lifelong fan of the mystery and thriller genres, Blake loves to hear from you, so please feel free to visit www.blakepierceauthor.com to learn more and stay in touch.

Table of Contents

Prologue

Professor Ralph Henderson sighed, rubbed the bridge of his nose, and fished around in the pocket of his coat for his car keys. It had been a long evening of marking English papers, and either his students were getting more stupid or he was getting more tired of the job. He was more than ready to prop himself up in bed for the night with a small glass of whiskey and one of the classics.

The Georgetown parking garage was almost empty, most of the other faculty members having had enough sense to go home long ago. It was chilly and gloomy, the electric strip lights flickering overhead as moths bumped into them with suicidal intent. Henderson cut across the empty spaces, taking a shortcut to his car. He briefly trifled with the idea of stopping off somewhere for a takeout coffee on the way back. Or would it be better just to get home as soon as possible, to the safety and warmth of one's own domain?

His footsteps echoed with an eerie resonance through the garage, the concrete ceiling and the concrete floor throwing the sounds back and forth. It was on nights like these that the garage transformed into a different kind of beast. A place where unsavory types might lurk in the shadows, ready to pounce. The kind of thinking that you couldn't shake, even when you repeatedly told yourself you were an adult and shouldn't be afraid of the dark anymore.

Mind you, there was a good reason to be nervous tonight. The campus had been buzzing with news of a murder that had taken place right there, under their own noses. A student that Henderson had known. Maybe that was the reason the hairs stood up on the back of his neck as he crossed the garage, and why he couldn't help but dart furtive and wide-eyed glances into the shadows, trying to see if there was someone hiding within.

He tried to distract himself. There was more to think about. There was a kid he'd had to throw out of the class for failing yet another paper. It was so frustrating to teach—to see these kids with so much potential getting caught up in parties and not taking their studies seriously. It was with regret that Henderson had had to flunk him, but he felt more than justified now after getting an email from the student.

Full of vitriol, the email was borderline threatening. Apparently, the kid didn't appreciate being kicked out and wanted to make sure that Henderson knew it. As if such a gesture was somehow going to get him reinstated to the course. Ha! The kid had a lot to learn about life, and about how people reacted to the way you treated them.

Henderson reached the car and fumbled with his keys, his fingers thick and slow from having written out so many comments while grading the students. He cursed himself, a shaking taking over his hands, driven by the isolation of the parking garage at night. He was being silly. He was a grown man, for god's sake, and he walked through this garage in the light of day without ever a second thought.

Anyway, he thought to himself darkly, if anyone was going to be after him, it would be that angry student. And he wasn't smart enough to stalk a professor in the dark of a parking garage. He was the kind of kid who sent angry emails and left a trail. Nothing to worry about, really. Henderson would report it to the dean tomorrow, and that would be that.

What was that noise? A footstep? Something was wrong here. He had been dismissing his fears all this time, but now he was less sure. The prickling feeling on the back of Henderson's neck increased, something like a premonition, but before he could turn, his head was hitting the car window with a sharp crash.

Henderson barely had time to register this fact and the flooding pain coming from his nose before the hand on the back of his head smashed it into the side of the car again. He was slipping lower, taken down by the shock and the injury, his body going limp. He tried to twist away a little, his briefcase flying forgotten to the floor, but he couldn't fight the next blow, or the next. Over and over his head hit the red chassis, his temple, the top of an eye socket, his jaw just below the ear.

He felt the damage with a kind of detached shock. The crack of a bone breaking. The thought of bruises blossoming across his face, then of cuts and abrasions, then of something more serious. All he could think, stupidly, was that his face was going to be ruined. All he had time to think before it was seemingly over.

The gripping hand released him, and Henderson sank unceremoniously to the floor, hitting a shoulder on the way down. He barely felt it, against all the rest. He was twisted enough now to groggily turn his head and look, though his vision was blurred. Maybe from the blows. Maybe from blood falling into his eyes. Maybe because his eye socket had to be broken, at the very least.

Who was that? A vague shape, a whisper only, as if it were a ghost that stood over him and not a man. But it was a man. It had to be a man. If only he could make out just who—but Henderson's consciousness was slipping out of him like sand through his fingers, and he could no longer hold on. Something was flowing out of him, leaving him cold and empty. He knew it was almost over. The world was going black around him, the watery shape above watching in silence.

The shadow stretched above him and lifted his head one last time and slammed it down into the concrete, an impact that Henderson barely even sensed before he tumbled down headfirst into that blackness.

The job was done.

He would not wake up again.

Chapter One

Zoe traced cracks across the arm of the leather chair, seeing how their pattern revealed a tale of aging, of so many different hands and arms lying on this exact spot. She couldn't decide whether that was a comfort, an indication of experience, or just gross. Who knew what kind of germs lurked within this fabric?

"Zoe?" Dr. Lauren Monk prompted her, from a similarly comfortable chair placed opposite her.

Zoe looked up guiltily. "Sorry, was I supposed to answer that?"

Dr. Monk sighed, tapping her pen against a pad of paper in her hand. Despite the recorder sitting on the desk which archived all of their sessions, it seemed that Dr. Monk was still a fan of traditional methods. "Let's change tack for a moment," she said. "We've had a few sessions together now, haven't we, Zoe? I'm noticing that you sometimes have trouble with social cues."

Ah. That. Zoe shrugged, trying to give off an air of indifference. "I do not always understand the ways in which people seem to react."

"Or the ways in which they expect you to react?"

Zoe shrugged again, her gaze traveling toward the window. Then she mentally slapped herself; she was supposed to be taking an active part in these sessions, not acting like a moody teenager. "My logic is different from their logic."

"Why do you think that is?"

Zoe knew why she was the way she was, or at least thought she did. The numbers. The numbers that were everywhere she looked, every moment of the day. They told her even now what prescription Dr. Monk wore in her glasses (barely strong enough to require any kind of aid), that there was half a millimeter of dust on the certificate frames on the wall but only a quarter of a millimeter on the psychology degree (indicating a stronger sense of pride in this than her other achievements), and that Dr. Monk had written down exactly seven words during their conversation so far.

She wanted to say it, or at least some parts of her did. She still had not admitted to Dr. Monk that she had an ability that no one else seemed to. No one except for the occasional serial killer, if the case she had worked a month or so ago was anything to go by.

But there was another part of her, still the stronger part, that could not bear to admit anything at all.

"I was just born this way," Zoe said.

Dr. Monk nodded, but did not write anything down. Apparently, this was not a significant enough answer. "How does it feel when you miss those social cues? Does it bother you?"

Maybe it was the fact that they had done enough sessions together now for the initial awkwardness to fade away. Maybe it was just the freedom of talking to someone with whom she had no real professional or personal connection. Either way, Zoe's mouth blurted out a truth that her mind had kept hidden from now, without her conscious permission. "Shelley finds it so easy."

Zoe cursed herself immediately. What kind of thing to say was that? Now they would spend the rest of the session digging into this jealousy she felt toward Shelley, instead of working on real problems. Until this moment she had not even really acknowledged to herself that the envy was there.

"Agent Shelley Rose," Dr. Monk said, consulting her notes from a previous afternoon in her office. "You feel more comfortable with her than your previous partners, you indicated to me previously. But you feel jealousy towards her. Can you expand on that?"

Zoe took a breath. Of course she could, though she did not want to. Reluctantly, she studied her own fingers, thinking it best to just get it over with. "Shelley has a way with people. She talks them into admitting things. And they like her. Not just suspects. Everyone."

"Do you feel that people don't like you, Zoe?"

Zoe shifted uncomfortably. This was all her own fault. She shouldn't have said something like that. Admitting a weakness was an invitation for someone to dig into it. This was why she had not mentioned the numbers yet. Even if this therapist had been suggested by Dr. Applewhite, her most trusted friend and mentor, that didn't mean that Zoe could trust her with her deepest and darkest secret. "I do not have many friends. Partners usually request to transfer away from me," she admitted instead.

"Do you think this is linked to your struggle with social cues?"

The woman was asking an obvious question. "That, and other things."

"What things?"

The obvious question. Zoe groaned inwardly. She had set herself up for that trap. "My job is difficult. I am gone often. There is not much time to put down roots."

Dr. Monk nodded thoughtfully. She was smiling encouragingly, as if Zoe was really getting somewhere. The part of her that craved the positive attention and affection she had never received from her mother thrilled at that, even though she did not want it to. Being in therapy was, so far, only serving to highlight all of her flaws. "What about Shelley? Does she have roots?"

Zoe nodded, swallowing down an unbidden lump. "She has a husband and a young daughter. Amelia. She talks about her a lot."

Dr. Monk put her pen to her lips, tapping it three times meaningfully. "You want a family of your own."

Zoe looked up sharply, then remembered not to be surprised that a therapist could discern the truest thoughts lurking behind whatever else you said. "Yes," she said, simply. There was no point in denying it. "But I am very far from that point."

"When we met for our first session, you told me you'd been on a date." Dr. Monk did not have to check through her notes for this, Zoe saw. "He contacted you, didn't he? Did you reply?"

Zoe shook her head no. "He has sent me a few emails, and tried to call. I did not answer."

"Why is that?"

Zoe shrugged. She couldn't exactly say. She reached up self-consciously to touch a few strands of her brown hair, kept cropped short for convenience rather than fashion. There were many things about her that were not perhaps conventionally attractive, and she knew that, even if she didn't exactly understand how other people saw her. "Maybe because the first date was awkward. I was too distracted. I could not focus on what he was saying. I was boring."

"But he didn't think so, did he? This . . .?"

"John."

"This John, he seems interested. He keeps trying to get in touch. That's a good sign."

Zoe nodded. There was nothing else that she could say. Dr. Monk was making sense, even if she hated to admit it.

"Let me tell you what I see," Dr. Monk continued. "You have expressed to me that Shelley has the kind of life you want. She is happily married with a child, doing well in her career, has skills that you don't have. We will always be jealous of those who can do things we can't. That's human nature. The important thing is not to let it consume you, and to focus on the things that you can achieve."

She waited for Zoe to nod again, to give an indication that she was listening, before she continued.

"Things don't happen on their own. Or to put it another way, it's unlikely that you are going to get married if you never go on any dates. My advice to you is to give John a call, and go out for that second date. Maybe it won't turn out so well. Maybe it will turn out great. The only way to find out is to give it a try."

"You think I should marry John?" Zoe frowned.

"I think you should go on a date with him." Dr. Monk smiled. "And if he doesn't work out, I think you should go on a date with someone else. That's how you work towards your goals. One step at a time."

Zoe was not entirely convinced, but she nodded all the same. Besides, she had something important to take care of now. "I think that is the end of our time."

Dr. Monk laughed. "That's my line," she said, getting up to escort Zoe to the door. "And don't think I am so easily distracted. Next session, we'll circle back to this issue of social cues and seeing things differently from how others do. We'll get to the bottom of it, even if you aren't ready to be fully honest with me."

Zoe avoided her therapist's eyes as she headed out of the office, not wanting to betray the hope she had held that Dr. Monk really would forget.

Chapter Two

At least lunch was something for Zoe to get excited about. It had been a long while since she had been able to meet with her mentor in person, and she had been looking forward to it. It was enough to get her through the therapy session and out the other side, knowing that there was something good coming.

Dr. Francesca Applewhite, a professor of mathematics who had worked at Zoe's college, had turned out to be one of the best introductions Zoe had ever had in her life. Back then, still a teenager and way out of her depth in the social atmosphere of the dorms, she had been skeptical about one more meeting with one more specialist. But it turned out that the doctor understood her completely—saw that she had a special gift, something which needed to be nurtured. They had started with private tutoring, designed to lift her skills to another academic level. Everything else had developed from there.

"Doctor," Zoe greeted, reaching their table and dropping herself down into the free chair. Dr. Applewhite had no doubt been there for some time, judging by the half-drunk cup of coffee and the worn paperback in her hands. Zoe could not help but notice that the streaks of gray were gaining strand by strand against her once-dark hair, a stark contrast to the version of the doctor in her memory of that first time.

Dr. Applewhite slipped a bookmark between the pages and put it to one side, smiling as she looked up. "My favorite graduate. How is the Bureau treating you?"

She had good reason to ask the question. It had been her suggestion, after all, that put Zoe on the path toward law enforcement. After her colleague, one of Zoe's math teachers, had connected them, Zoe's whole life had changed. She knew exactly who she had to thank for that.

"Good. My new partner is going well," Zoe said. She picked up the menu to scan the items, but she barely needed to. She already knew what she was going to order. A scan of the column and row sizes told her that nothing new had been added, and they always met for lunch at this place.

Dr. Applewhite leaned over to grab the attention of a waiter, and while the doctor watched him walking over, Zoe watched her instead. She remembered that first meeting. How Dr. Applewhite had shown an actual interest in what Zoe had to say, one of the few people in her life who had actually really listened to her. The older woman had put on several pounds since that time, but had never lost an ounce of the compassion she showed to a young woman who had no idea of her place in the world.

Their relationship had grown over time. Zoe was slow to trust, slow to let her in. But eventually she had had to take a chance, to admit her secret. To tell her about the numbers.

It hadn't been easy. After so many years of Zoe's mother telling her that her gifts were given her by the devil, she had found the words caught in her throat many times. But Dr. Applewhite had been excited, not appalled, to learn of Zoe's abilities. From then on, their bond had only strengthened.

"How about Dr. Monk?" Dr. Applewhite asked after Zoe had placed her order, her eyes twinkling slyly. "She told me you took me up on my recommendation."

Zoe couldn't contain a chuckle. "Checking up on me?"

"I always have to keep an eye on my favorites," Dr. Applewhite laughed. It was an ongoing joke between them. Dr. Applewhite was not, of course, supposed to have favorites. But in many ways, Zoe had helped her career just as much as Dr. Applewhite had set Zoe on the way to hers. Dr. Applewhite had ended up specializing in the study of synesthesia with regards to math, and now mentored a number of others who had the same abilities that Zoe did. More or less, anyway.

"The sessions are going well," Zoe acknowledged. "Dr. Monk has some good insights. I can see why you like her."

"She has a very good reputation. Any progress you can share with me? Or is it all too personal?"

Zoe shrugged, studying the two inches of water in the bottom of the vase on their table, which would not be enough to sustain the two chrysanthemum stems for long. The internal calculations of how long it would take for a total wilt distracted her enough to allow her to say what was on her mind. "She said I should go on more dates."

Dr. Applewhite grinned heartily, her own wedding ring glittering in the light from the sun as she raised her coffee cup to her lips. "She could be right."

"I really do not think it will be the solution to all my problems," Zoe huffed, lifting the fresh cup of coffee brought by the waiter to her lips.

"Maybe not all of them, but some," Dr. Applewhite said, serious now. "I'm not saying that you have to feel bad about who you are. You're functional—more than that. You have turned it into an advantage in your work. Others aren't as capable as you are. I just worry about you. You know I do."

Zoe nodded. "I appreciate that," she said. She figured that, with all things considered, Dr. Applewhite might be the only person in the world to actually worry about her. That was a comfort, to have at least one person.

Before she could complete the thought, and even go so far as to take the recommendation to call John seriously, her cell rang in her pocket. Zoe grabbed it out and answered the call, seeing Shelley's name on the display.

"Special Agent Zoe Prime."

"Hey, Z. Hope you're not doing something nice right now."

Zoe sighed, looking down at her half-finished plate of food. Not that she had even really noticed the taste, with her mind on other things. "I take it we have a case."

"I'll meet you at HQ in thirty minutes. The chief says this is a big one."

Zoe offered Dr. Applewhite an apologetic smile, but the doctor was already waving her away. "Go do your duty, Agent. But there's one more thing I have to tell you…" Dr. Applewhite hesitated, taking a breath. She seemed reluctant to speak, but forged on, looking down at Zoe's half-empty plate as she did. "One of the others in my research group—another synesthete. We thought he was doing better, but… I'm sorry to say, he killed himself last week. Without a support network beyond myself, he was struggling. Humans need other humans around us, to help us emotionally. All of us do. Even those who think a bit differently."

Zoe paused, staring down into her coffee cup and the several millimeters by which it had been underfilled, leaning back against the chair for support. She had never gone to meet any of Dr. Applewhite's "research group"—test subjects, Zoe called them in her head when she was being unkind—but all the same, it was a blow to hear. Someone like her, who wanted to die for the sole reason that he was exactly like her. That was something to swallow, all right.

She picked up her bag mechanically, walking away without really seeing anything around herself. In her head she was reframing. Thinking back on Dr. Monk's comments. *Work towards your goals. One step at a time.*

What did she have in her life, really? One mentor, who served as the closest thing to a mother figure she was ever going to find. A partner—Shelley—who was the closest thing she had to a friend. Two cats, Euler and Pythagoras—and though she loved them both, she knew that it was in the very nature of cats that they would be just fine if she was gone and they lived with someone else. A career that seemed to be on the rocks more than it was on the up and up, even if right now was one of the better times. A small apartment to call her own.

And a condition, or an ability, or whatever you wanted to call it, that made her so different it drove people like her to kill themselves.

It was a sobering thought to confront.

Chapter Three

Zoe strode along the corridors of the vast FBI HQ building in Washington, DC, heading toward the particular briefing room where Shelley had said she would be waiting. Buildings like this were soothing for Zoe: built long enough ago but with enough planning and precision that each floor was easy to predict and navigate.

The J. Edgar Hoover building had been built with intent. Although from the outside it was square and gray, the kind of architecture people described as an eyesore, the blocky, geometric composition was exactly what Zoe loved about it. The corridors branched off in the exact same way no matter where you got off the elevator, and the rooms were numbered in a logical way. Room 406, quite naturally, was the sixth door that you would come to after getting off on the fourth floor. That was immeasurably pleasing. Not all buildings were created equal.

Sure enough, Shelley was already sitting in the briefing room, studying notes and color photographs placed at neat intervals along a boardroom table. She looked up and smiled as Zoe entered.

Zoe could not quite figure out how Shelley, with a young child at home and no particular advantage in distance from her home, could beat her to the HQ. Not only that, but how she could be neatly dressed in a suit that fit her curvy yet slim frame, accentuating the angles between her hips and waist and breasts, without a speck of the normal dirt one would expect to accumulate around an infant. Even how she could be perfectly made up, with a slight hint of pink lipstick on her lips, and her blonde hair tied just-so into a chic chignon. But there it was.

Their superior, Special Agent in Charge Leo Maitland, stood at the front of the room, waiting with the coiled impatience of a jaguar on the hunt. He was an Army vet with a soldier's bearing, and after a successful career through the ranks he had come home to switch to law enforcement. That had all been fifteen years ago, but the graying hair at his temples gave no indication that he was any less the fighter he had once been. He stood at six foot three, with a forty-five-inch chest and fifteen-inch biceps that still strained at the hems of his uniform.

"Ah, Special Agent Prime," he said. "Welcome. I've handed out the briefing notes to your partner. Please take a seat and go over them."

Zoe sat as she was bidden, setting down a takeout coffee in front of Shelley. It had become a habit of theirs. Zoe provided the coffee, and Shelley would provide all the polite conversation that was needed during the case. Each of them taking care of something that they could actually manage.

"Special Agent Rose has all the information, but I'll give you an overview. We have two bodies on our hands already, and this looks like a local case, so you won't need to travel." Maitland folded his arms over his chest, causing the material of his suit to visibly strain at the shoulders. "We'll be under some pressure from the local press given that one of the victims was high-profile in the community. You are no doubt also familiar with the urgency of preventing a third death and having the term 'serial killer' attached by journalists."

Zoe nodded. That kind of reporting could cause hysteria and end up impeding the case. It was also likely to spread the news further—and that meant more national or even international press to deal with. FBI agents were used to dealing with high-pressure situations, but that did not mean they were welcome. Particularly for Zoe, who would be counting microphones and analyzing the lengths of television camera cables rather than concentrating on her press conference speech.

"Given your lateness…" Maitland continued. Zoe felt her mouth beginning to open in protest, but she clamped it shut. She had arranged to take some time off this morning for her brunch, exchanging some of the many, many hours of unpaid overtime she had worked. She was hardly late. But one did not argue with the Special Agent in Charge of the J. Edgar Hoover Building. "I have already briefed your partner. I will leave her to dispense the details to you. Given your proclivity for math, we thought this would be an excellent fit for your skillset. Don't let me down."

Maitland swept out of the room without pausing to look back. Zoe noted his hand straying immediately to his pocket as he left the room, and figured the inch-thick bulge was likely a cell phone. He was a busy man, with calls to make and further briefings to give. It wasn't likely that they would see him much until the case was done—unless they messed something up, in which case he was liable to come down like the figurative ton of bricks.

Given Maitland's size, and that a ton was two thousand pounds, he wasn't really like a ton of bricks at all. More like a tenth of that value.

"Two victims," Shelley said, grabbing Zoe's attention without so much as a polite triviality to start the conversation. She was starting to know Zoe better, and she must have realized by now that such comments would make no positive difference to their relationship. Zoe had noticed at least a seventy percent decrease in small talk since they had begun working together. "Both of them in our own backyard. DC metro area."

"I hope not in either of our actual backyards. As federal agents, you would think we might notice."

Shelley's eyes flashed with a spark as she nudged Zoe in the ribs. "Was that an actual joke? What's in this coffee?"

"I was with an old friend this morning. I suppose it put me in a good mood."

"Then I'm sorry to break that." Shelley pointed to the two victim files, spread out carefully and separated in a deliberate way. "This is the first victim, from about a week ago. He was a young grad student, found on the grounds of the Georgetown campus. His head was bashed in with a heavy object—forensics say that it was probably a bat."

"Six days," Zoe murmured, her eyes scanning the file. She picked up his information: six feet tall, one hundred eighty pounds, twenty-three years old.

"Sorry, yes." Shelley was evidently still getting used to the precision that Zoe expected, even if they were finding it easy to settle in in other ways. "The second victim was last night. An English professor at Georgetown, his head was smashed repeatedly against the side of his own car until irreparable cranial damage had been inflicted."

"The college is the connection."

"Not just that." Shelley shuffled the photographs, drew out overhead shots that showed the crime scene in full. "Both of them had their shirts ripped open—and I mean ripped, with some violence. It seems the act of killing wasn't enough to sate the killer's anger. Then there are these . . . well, see for yourself."

Zoe all but snatched the images from Shelley's hands. She had already begun to recognize the form of the markings scribbled across both men's torsos, and a closer look confirmed it. They had both been emblazoned with complex mathematical equations—complex enough that Zoe pulled out a chair and sank into it without taking her eyes away.

"Have these been shown to any potential witnesses? Friends, faculty members, students?"

"In the case of the first victim, yes. The local cops showed the image around. Heavily cropped to just the equation itself, of course. They just finished circulating the other shot this morning, though we may still be able to dig up a few more leads, I suppose."

"And?"

Shelley shrugged. "No one knows what it means."

Zoe knew well enough that the math department at Georgetown had a good stock of professionals, and if they couldn't figure it out, that meant that this was some serious kind of equation. "It looks like quantum math."

"That's what a few of the professors said. But they don't recognize it as anything that any of them have seen before, or been working on."

Zoe continued staring at the equation, her mind racing along and through all the complex signs and numbers and letters, trying to find at least an entrance into the pattern. "What other leads do we have?"

Shelley sifted through a few more pages. "I was just getting there when you came in. Let me see . . . the student's roommates and friends have all been questioned, as well as his family and teaching staff. He was in an area of the campus which isn't covered by cameras, right in a dead spot."

"Convenient," Zoe sighed. She wished that just once, they would get hold of a case that had been committed in full sight of witnesses or caught on camera. Of course, they didn't usually call in the FBI for the ones that were easy to solve.

"As for the professor, looks like there were only cameras at the entrance to the parking lot. So many people come in and out of there all day, and we don't have eyes on one of the pedestrian exits at all. Nothing suspicious caught on camera."

"No leads at all," Zoe noted, propping her chin on one hand as she went over the equation for the seventeenth time already. Slower, faster, it wasn't making much difference. This was like nothing she had ever come across. Far beyond the level that she had studied during her own time in college.

She switched to the other one, the professor. It seemed just the same. What was this?

"What do you want to do first?" Shelley asked, completing her own study of the files.

"Just a second." Zoe had not even taken the time to check the second victim's particulars yet, but there was time for that. She took out her notebook and pen and started writing, making quick and sharp indentations on the page as she began to sketch out an initial working. Greek letters, lines, brackets, downward-pointing triangles—all symbols in quantum math had an equivalent meaning that would reveal a number. M divided by t" minus t', one divided by s' then added to one divided by s", and so on and so forth, all to find the value of B^I which could later be inserted back into another line of the equation to work out the value of another figure.

The workings started easily enough. If the value of M was equal to the value of r', then the first two lines made perfect sense; but then the third line disrupted it all, and appeared to give a totally different value for M. Fine; she worked it through another way. Perhaps M was, in fact, double the value of r', which still made enough sense there, and made the third line work—but by the sixth line, the value of M had to be shown to reach zero, and there again it all made no sense.

When Zoe looked up again, she had no idea how much time had passed. At some point, Shelley had sat down opposite her, and was thumbing through something on the screen of her cell.

"This does not make any sense," Zoe announced.

Shelley looked up, lifting a carefully shaped eyebrow. "You can't work them out?"

Zoe's lips flattened into a thin line before she could make herself admit it. "I cannot work them out *yet*," she said. "Maybe we are missing some kind of clue. This is definitely all of it? There was not something written on their backs, or arms, or elsewhere?"

"I know as much as you know," Shelley said. "I've been reading up on the professor. Nothing stands out from his academic history, or from what I can see of his personal life that has made it online."

"Check the photos again," Zoe suggested, handing her a bundle and picking up some for herself. She pored over the shots, her eyes taking in the angles of bones, the degree at which a leg had bent in death, the length of the rips in their shirts versus the visible strength of the material and its stitching. Nowhere could she see any connection. Not in their heights, weight, their ages—and no hint of any other ink slashed across their skin.

The worrying thing, of course, was that mathematical patterns became easier to predict the more data you had. Two numbers could seem unconnected, any number of possibilities between them, too many to decide on a definite course. Three numbers, well, that would allow one to make more of a case, begin a formula. But that would require another death.

And they certainly didn't want another death.

"I've got nothing," Shelley said, shaking her head.

"Swap," Zoe suggested, handing her bundle over and taking Shelley's in return. "The only thing of note is the angle of the impact on the first victim's head. The attacker was a little shorter, probably five nine."

And again, it was the same. The same frustrating nothing. No hint of ink on clothing, no trailing off of the numbers underneath fabric, nothing in the general vicinity. The parking garage spaces were not numbered, and nor were there numbers on the walls, on the concrete columns holding up the ceiling, on the grass near where the student was found.

Nothing.

Zoe gave up, shaking her head. "I need to see the professor's body," she said. "It is the only way we are going to spot something that the photographs do not already tell us."

"Great," Shelley said. It was possible that she was being sarcastic; Zoe had always had a hard time telling the difference. "Then let's go take a close look at a dead guy."

Chapter Four

Zoe tapped her fingers on the steering wheel as they drove over to the local coroner, glancing sideways at Shelley. There was something about this case that was already bothering her, and she had to voice the doubts that were creeping into her head before they became obsessive. "It's funny that Maitland knew I would want to work on a math-based case. I have never discussed with him that I enjoy working with numbers."

Shelley cleared her throat slightly, not turning to meet Zoe's eyes. "Well, I volunteered us for this one. I just happened to hear it coming in, and, well, the chief agreed we could take it."

Zoe digested this for a moment. She didn't usually get things from her boss just because she asked for them. "Just like that? You did not need to persuade him?"

Shelley was twisting the pendant she wore, a gold arrow set with a diamond that she had inherited from her grandmother, around and around in her fingers. "I told him that since you were really good with math, we would be able to get a better start on it than anyone else."

Zoe resisted the urge to slam on the brakes, keeping the car steady and smooth. She focused on the road until the rushing in her head had slowed down, and spoke deliberately and calmly. "You said I was 'good with math'?"

"That's all I said, I swear. I didn't tell them the truth. Not about, you know, what you can do."

Shelley sounded apologetic, but that was not quite enough to make the roaring in Zoe's ears go away. Good with math. That was close to the truth, too close to be comfortable. It was almost an admission.

Maybe she had made a grave mistake, trusting Shelley to not give away her secret. But her partner had sworn, so many times over, that she would never reveal it to anyone without Zoe's consent. While she technically had still not done that, it was close. Too close.

"Look, it's fine, isn't it?" Shelley asked. Her voice had risen in pitch now. "I'm really sorry if you didn't want me to say that, but it's just a little piece of the way things really are. Not the whole picture. And anyone can be good at math, you know? It doesn't make you that much different."

Zoe's fingers tightened on the steering wheel, so tight the rubber grips made a quiet noise, and she worked her jaw stiffly. "It was not up to you to tell them that."

"I just—I didn't think it would be a big deal, to say that much." Shelley sighed, slumping back against the passenger seat headrest. "I messed up, I can see that now. I'm sorry. But after you solved our big case in Kansas, surely they would have to figure that you're good with numbers anyway. I know I can't tell anyone, and I won't, but I don't know why you feel you need to hide it."

Zoe gritted her teeth. Of course, Shelley didn't understand. Shelley hadn't been there. She hadn't been forced to pray by her bed on the cold floor all night, her mother shrieking and sermonizing about the devil's gift. She hadn't been scolded at school for her distraction, or made fun of and ostracized by the other children for the uncanny things she could tell just by looking at them.

She hadn't been there through every failed relationship Zoe had endured, misunderstood time and time again, left with nothing but the label "freak" and another broken heart.

"It is my secret to tell, or not, as I choose," she said firmly, once her heart was beating slow enough again that she could say the words instead of spit them, and Shelley had the wisdom to forgo a reply.

They pulled up outside the coroner's office and Zoe slammed the car door behind her, stalking over to the entrance. Then she stopped. It would do no good at all to go into the examination with this kind of energy hanging over her. She had to forget it, put it on a shelf inside her mind and come back to it later. For now, she had to be professional.

The coroner, a trim Asian woman in her mid-forties with sharp eyes and hair cut at a sharp ninety-degree bob in line with her chin, was obliging enough. She showed them the professor's body, and stood back respectfully while they made their examination.

Lying naked on the metal gurney, the man was reduced to nothing more than white meat. Take the sheet away, and it was hard for Zoe to connect and keep connected the lines between this hunk of dead flesh and the man it had been. Whoever he was had long gone. She could see it still, in the yellowed fingertips that spoke of a nicotine habit and the small inch-long impression over his left ear where he had spent years wearing ill-fitting glasses. But the essence, the being, whatever it was that had once filled this body and animated it, was nowhere to be found.

It was better that way. People distracted her. They hid their true selves behind words and gestures that she could not always understand. But bodies could not lie. They were as they were, no more and no less.

It didn't hurt, of course, that his face was gone. Smashed inward. The nose had been reduced to an entirely flat plane of the face, all the bumps and curves pressed against the inside of his skull now. The right side of the head, too, was cracked and squashed, bearing clear lines of impact. No one could have survived that. Even one of his eyes was gone.

The equation was there on his torso, written out sideways from the top of his chest to just below his navel. It was all as it seemed in the photographs—the full piece had been captured faithfully. Wearing uncomfortable white disposable gloves, Zoe turned over each of his arms and legs, and even hefted him onto his side with Shelley's assistance. Nowhere could they see any other trace of ink, or indeed any marking that could hint at being a missing part of the equation.

"They didn't miss anything," Shelley said out loud, confirming the growing frustration that was building in the center of Zoe's forehead.

"The other one." Zoe turned to look at the coroner. "We need to see the student as well."

The coroner shrugged, making a gesture that seemed to suggest she thought it pointless, and walked over to open another tray of the metal filing cabinet that served as a temporary resting place. She tugged it open with a long scraping sound of well-oiled metal on metal, and stepped back to allow them access to the resident.

The college student looked even younger than he had in the photographs, lying on the cold metal tray with all the blood drained out of his cheeks and the color with it. The top of his head was a mess, open and crushed inward. He was covered with a respectful sheet, but respect was only an obstacle in this case. Zoe stepped closer and tugged it aside, noting Shelley's reluctance to do so.

For a long second, Zoe stared, unable to comprehend what she was looking at. Then she briefly wondered if they had pulled out the wrong body, but she had recognized his face from the crime scene photos. Finally, disbelief reigned, and she turned on the coroner with a glower that had the other woman backing away.

"Where are the equations?" Zoe asked, her tone low and flat, menacing enough to tell anyone about the anger behind it.

"Well, we performed the autopsy," the coroner stuttered, feeling for a metal table behind her to steady herself. "We always wash the bodies to perform the autopsy."

"You scrubbed away the evidence."

Shelley stepped closer to lay a gentle hand on Zoe's arm, perhaps warning her to cool down. Zoe ignored it. She was seething, every muscle in her body wanting to explode in a burst of energy and throw something at the wall. Maybe at the coroner.

The only reason she didn't was that it was very clearly against the professional code of conduct. How could they have allowed something like this to happen?

"Who authorized the cleaning?" Shelley asked, her tone quiet and calm. She stepped forward, slightly in front of Zoe, as if shielding her.

The coroner fumbled for paperwork, still stuttering, her face gone pale. Zoe couldn't take any more. She stalked out of the room with a growl in the back of her throat, slamming the door behind her for good measure. It being a swing door, the movement lost some of its effect, but it released some of the tension in her body all the same.

Shelley joined her a couple minutes later, finding her pacing up and down at the end of the corridor.

"We should have them written up for tampering with evidence," Zoe said, as soon as Shelley was close enough to hear.

"They were within the scope of their instructions," Shelley sighed, shrugging her shoulders. "The photographer felt they had captured everything. We're just going to have to take their word for it."

"They should be punished anyway. Do they not have common sense? It was *clearly* evidence. And the lead investigators not having even seen the body yet!"

"Well, in fairness, this was a local case when they did the autopsy, not a federal one. What's done is done. We just have to work with what we have."

Shelley was being rational; too rational. Zoe didn't like it. She wanted a justification for the frustration she felt, dammit, a common feeling between the two of them. She hated being made to feel like she was the freak with the problem. Things being done incorrectly was a problem. People were supposed to do the jobs they were paid for. That was how society *worked*.

"Something like that should have been obviously important," Zoe said, trying one last attempt at lulling Shelley into her own rage.

It was not to be. "We've got to keep moving anyway," Shelley said, stepping outside and looking back to make sure Zoe was following her. "Should we go talk to the professor's wife next?"

Zoe nodded, giving up. Maybe she was overreacting. She had been told that she could do that, on occasion.

There was more to this case than the physical evidence on the bodies. Of course, the math was tantalizing, as was the target of a respected university. But there was always another story to be heard from the family of the victims, the people who knew them.

Perhaps Mrs. Henderson would be able to shed some light on her husband's death—and get this frustrating case wrapped up sooner rather than later.

Chapter Five

Shelley took the driver's seat, an uncommon occurrence when she was driving with her partner. Shelley knew that Zoe was normally carsick, but today she was so preoccupied with her equations that she hardly seemed to notice the roads flashing by. She wasn't even clutching at her seatbelt, her usual tell for discomfort.

Shelley glanced over whenever she had a chance—waiting at intersections or paused in a line of traffic. What Zoe was scribbling down frantically across multiple pages of her notebook made no sense at all to her. They might as well have been hieroglyphics.

Zoe had a real gift when it came to numbers, but there were other sides to that too. A single-minded obsession could take over at times, like now. As much as Shelley wanted to help, she had no idea what was required—and Zoe wasn't about to tell her. She was like that fairly often, too. Quiet, closed off. Shelley had heard the stories about her previous partners, and it wasn't hard to extrapolate that she maybe had given up on trusting people with her thoughts a long time ago.

Zoe was used to working alone. If she had her way, Shelley was going to change that. It just might take her a long while to get there. In the meantime, she would have to keep prompting her and reminding her to share her thoughts.

Just maybe not about math. Shelley could trust her to work on the math alone.

The English professor lived across town, in one of the flashier suburbs, white-painted houses with wide lawns and matching white fences. Shelley pulled up outside, killing the engine, and waited for Zoe to notice.

She didn't even look up.

There were times when Shelley felt that she needed to tread carefully around Zoe—to handle her with the utmost care. With kid gloves. Which was somewhat ironic, given that Shelley spent all of her time at home being a parent. There were more than a few times that she felt she was doing the same thing at work, even if Zoe was the older of the two of them.

"We're here," Shelley said, softly, not wanting to startle Zoe out of the middle of the calculations she was working on.

Zoe's pen hesitated in midair, and she looked up at last. She seemed surprised to be anywhere other than the coroner's office parking lot. "I just need to finish..."

Shelley raised an eyebrow. "Z, is it going to take less than two minutes to finish? Because if not, maybe we should go and talk to the professor's wife, and come back to the equation later."

Zoe sighed noisily, but seemed to agree. She stowed her notebook away in a pocket and got out of the car, which Shelley took as a signal to do the same. She revised her earlier thought: dealing with Zoe wasn't exactly like dealing with a child. More like a surly teenager, at times.

Mrs. Henderson seemed to have been waiting for them, or at least for someone. She was dressed neatly in a dark floral dress, the muted colors conveying something of what she was going through. Her eyes were rimmed with red, but open and sharp, assessing Shelley and Zoe within moments of their meeting at the threshold.

"I'm Special Agent Shelley Rose, and this is Special Agent Zoe Prime. We'd like to come in and talk about your husband, Mrs. Henderson."

The woman nodded, gesturing them inward, stepping out of the way so that she could close the door after they entered. The house was furnished in an understated classic style, all dark wood and comfortable cushions and throws. Mrs. Henderson led them through into a lounge area, where Shelley gratefully accepted the offer of coffee on both Zoe's and her own behalf.

"She's taking it very well," Shelley murmured, casting an eye around their new setting. It was neat, not a single item out of place. No dust on the low, marble-topped coffee table or the dark sideboard weighed down with mementos and tchotchkes. Several pieces of fresh fruit rested in a burnished bowl in the center of the table. It looked more like a television set than a home that was actually lived in.

Maybe Mrs. Henderson's way of dealing with her grief was to clean and tidy the home, ready for visitors. It wouldn't be completely unusual. Shelley had seen it before. It was tied to denial—the thought that if she just made sure that everything was perfect, her husband might come back in through the door.

The busywork, too, put off the grief.

A framed photograph sat on the mantelpiece: the professor and his wife, in happier times. Shelley looked at it and tried not to see the horrific mess that the professor's head had been turned into.

"Seventeen figurines," Zoe muttered. Shelley followed her gaze to the sideboard and knew that Zoe was doing what she always did: looking for numbers. In this case, however, they had already taken on a new significance. She was looking for a clue that would lead to a breakthrough with the equations.

The mistress of the house returned after only a few minutes, carrying a tray laden with three hot cups of coffee. The dainty porcelain design of Mrs. Henderson's cup was offset by the plain practicality of the other two. Two personalities, coming to bear on the contents of a home. Maybe a statement that the visitors she had received today were not worthy of the best china.

"This must have come as a great shock to you," Shelley said, lifting her cup and blowing gently across the surface of the coffee before taking a sip. Questions or statements like this, open and inviting, often encouraged more information to spill forth. The kind of information that you might not even think to ask for otherwise.

"Oh, yes." Mrs. Henderson sighed deeply, settling back into the armchair which must have been her habitual place. "I still can't quite believe it. My Ralph, gone just like that. And so violently, too. I just can't fathom it."

"Can you think of a reason behind the level of violence, Mrs. Henderson?"

The older woman closed her eyes briefly, a hand fluttering up to her forehead. It was adorned still with a plain gold wedding band, alongside a more elaborate concoction of small diamonds. Perhaps an engagement ring, decades old. "At first I thought they meant to steal something. His car, or his wallet. But the police said nothing was gone."

"The psychologists tell us that there's evidence of great rage in the scene. That kind of anger, well, it usually comes from knowing someone personally. Is there anyone you can think of? Someone who would be angry with your husband, enough to wish him harm?"

An embroidered handkerchief came up to dab at her eyes, the ringed hand lifting to brush away a strand of her mousey brown hair. "I can't think of it. I mean, Ralph was—he was *Ralph.* He never hurt a fly. He got on well with his colleagues, was liked by his students. We have a few friends in the neighborhood who would come over for dinner now and then. He never so much as argued with strangers. There was nothing controversial about him. Everyone loved him!"

"All right, so no known enemies," Shelley said, nodding encouragingly even though she felt frustrated by the answer. It was always better to have somewhere to go next. "Through his whole career, do you think? He never had any trouble at all?"

Mrs. Henderson sniffed, shrugging her shoulders up and down. "Well, there was always something small," she said, though her tone indicated she thought it could not possibly mean anything. "He was a professor. There were students who didn't agree with their grades. Or those who flunked out for not attending class or turning in their work on time. They all think they ought to be given special treatment. But that's normal. Just part of the job. No one would kill over something like a *grade,* would they?"

Shelley could see that Mrs. Henderson was really asking the question—looking for reassurance. Sadly, Shelley knew that she could not give it to her. People killed for all kinds of reasons. There was not always rationality behind it. Sometimes it was simply the final straw that made them snap, on top of everything else.

Maybe it was an idea worth exploring. Rich, entitled kid given everything in life, suddenly starts to fail for the first time? Throws a fit driven by privilege? Or some down and out student with nothing left to live for—parents recently deceased, girlfriend broken up with him, lost his part-time job, and then a bad grade on top of all the rest? It was something to look into, at the very least.

"Let's hope not," she volunteered, along with a small smile intended to convey her sympathies. "Can you think of anything unusual that might have happened in the past days or weeks—even months?"

Mrs. Henderson shook her head, dabbing at her eyes again. "I've thought about it, over and over. Everything was just—normal. That's why it was such a shock. Totally out of the blue. I don't know why anyone would want to hurt my Ralph at all."

The woman was getting more and more distressed. Perhaps it would be prudent to wrap the interview up, leave her to her peace. "Is there anything else you can tell us—anything at all? It might not even seem relevant, but every little bit of information is another piece of the puzzle."

Mrs. Henderson shook her head helplessly.

"All right, one last question. Do you recall your husband ever talking about a student named Cole Davidson?"

"Not until his name was in the papers," Mrs. Henderson said. "That poor boy. Do you . . . do you think they are connected? They must be, mustn't they? Two murders within such a short space of time?"

"It's not useful for us to speculate at this stage." Shelley took a final gulp of her coffee, regretting the need to leave behind half of what had been a very decent cup. "But we'll be in touch if we can tell you more."

Shelley stood, then hesitated as Zoe joined her. "Mrs. Henderson, do you have someone to keep you company today?"

She nodded slowly, getting up to escort them to the door. "My daughter is flying home. She should be here by tonight."

That put Shelley's heart at ease. Leaving a woman alone with her grief never quite sat right, no matter how many family interviews she did. "Then we'll be in touch, Mrs. Henderson. In the meantime, try to get some rest."

They got back into the car, Zoe pulling out her notebook immediately to start scribbling again. Shelley wondered if she had even heard a word of the interview, or if she had immediately dismissed it as useless and spent the entire time thinking about numbers.

Whichever it was, Shelley couldn't get mad. Right now, the equations were the only real clues they had. As they drove back to base, Shelley couldn't help but worry that they would not find anything of more value that would break the case open. With Zoe so fixated on the numbers, it was going to be up to Shelley to find something else that would make a difference.

The problem was figuring out where to look.

Chapter Six

Zoe resented every moment of wasted time spent on the walk through the building, from the parking lot to the room they had taken over for their investigation. Nearly five hundred steps of distance that could have been spent on working. Nice as it was to be working on something that had happened, as Shelley put it, in their own backyard, Zoe was already getting irritable. The equations were refusing to give up their secrets to her, remaining obtuse and opaque.

As soon as she reached the table, Zoe sat down and resumed her notes, trying to work through every element of the professor's equation, bit by bit. His was the one they had seen in person, after all, the one that they could be sure was whole.

"I'm going to go through his faculty email account," Shelley announced, dumping her bag onto a chair and digging out her phone.

"Is that necessary?" Zoe asked, wrinkling her nose. There was no point in rushing around after some kind of clue like that. The answer was in the equations, not in the professor's personal life. It had to be. There was no link between Cole Davidson and this English professor, not without the equations.

"I'm not good at math, so I can't help you work through the numbers on this one," Shelley pointed out. "Something Mrs. Henderson said made me think. It could always be something to do with a student. Someone who felt slighted in some way. It's possible that there are many people who knew both Cole and Professor Henderson from campus."

Zoe hesitated, her objections waiting on the tip of her tongue. She felt like it would be a waste of time, poking through a dead man's emails. But what did it matter? Shelley was right—she couldn't help with the equations. And maybe it was time that Zoe started trusting her to investigate things in her own way.

Maybe, also, it would be good for Zoe if this case was solved off the back of a disgruntled email, rather than through the numbers. After Shelley had pointed out to their superiors that Zoe was good with math, Zoe wasn't exactly at pains to prove it. In fact, it would be better if she could pass that off as a partner's misplaced confidence.

But not, of course, if it compromised the case. Stopping the killer was still the most important thing.

Zoe returned her attention to the equations while Shelley called the university to get the access she needed. The thing was, she had gone about as far as she could go—with both of them. It was true that there was still the possibility of something missed on the student's body, but they had checked the professor for themselves.

So, what was she missing?

There was another possibility, of course: that she simply wasn't advanced enough to solve it. There was a difference between being able to see numbers—distances, dimensions, angles—and being able to solve quantum math problems. There were other skills involved, skills that other people spent their whole lives developing. Zoe might have had a gift, but she had devoted it to the pursuit of killers, not to the study of math.

Which brought another idea to her mind.

She got up, leaving Shelley still chatting with a receptionist on her cell, and carried a sheaf of photographs down the hall to the elevator. Up two floors, and down an identical corridor to the one she had left—except that the rooms on this floor had rather more power exuding from each of them.

Zoe took a breath before knocking on her boss's door. How many times had she been summoned here, to be chewed out for losing another partner or discharging her firearm?

But this was not like those times, and she entered when bidden, trying not to feel nervous.

With his imposing frame and larger than average musculature, it was easy to see how Special Agent in Charge Maitland would have been intimidating in the field. Criminals would have taken one look at him and then run.

Zoe was trying very hard not to feel the same.

"Sir," she said, hesitating in the doorframe.

Maitland looked up from his paperwork, then continued scrawling his signature at the bottom of a request. "Go on, Special Agent Prime. Don't wait out in the corridor all day."

Zoe stepped forward, letting the door close behind her with a little reluctance. She squared her shoulders, however, and faced him with the straight back she always felt inspired to uphold in his presence. "Sir, it is regarding the case Special Agent Rose and I are working on. The college kid and the professor, found with equations written on their bodies."

Despite the large caseload which must necessarily have gone through the DC field office, Maitland didn't skip a beat. "I know it. What do you need?"

"The equations are extremely high-level," Zoe said, feeling a little like a failure for even admitting they were too much for her. Still, it had to be done. Eyeing the neat ninety-degree angles of everything arranged on Maitland's desk, instead of watching his expression, she pushed herself onward. "I believe we would do better if we brought in a subject matter expert. Someone who could work on the equations from a professional mathematics standpoint."

Maitland nodded, then paused in his writing as he realized that she was done. "Do you have someone in mind? Special Agent Rose reminded us that you studied math once upon a time."

"I do, sir."

"Good." Maitland's attention returned to the paperwork, effectively dismissing her. "Permission granted. Have the paperwork turned in ASAP."

"Yes, sir." Zoe turned and almost fled for the door, happy to have such a positive outcome. She was not going to stick around and wait for him to change his mind, by any stretch of the imagination.

There was work to do—and someone very important to bring into the case.

Zoe waited expectantly, watching her mentor examine the images.

"These are ... disturbing." Dr. Applewhite shook her head, holding her lower lip between her teeth for three seconds as she slipped the photograph to the back of the pile in her hands and studied the next one. "I sometimes forget that you have to look at this kind of thing day in and day out. It must take a toll."

Zoe shrugged. "Dead bodies are dead. It is the not solving them that bothers me."

"And this is one that you haven't yet been able to solve." It was not a question. Zoe had already primed the doctor with the fact that she needed help. Dr. Applewhite knew that it was an open, ongoing case, and that permission had had to be sought for them to even be having this conversation. She understood also that time was of the essence. With every passing hour, it became less and less likely that they would find the person who did this.

The thing about homicides was that the first twenty-four hours were crucial. Everyone knew that. Forty-eight hours without an arrest, and you were starting to head into dangerous territory. The kind of cases that would become episodes of late-night TV shows.

The college kid had been dead for well over forty-eight hours.

"I need to know what it means," Zoe explained. "Right now, this is the only lead that we have. There does not seem to be any connection between the professor and the student, beyond the fact of their locations. No witnesses, no coverage of surveillance cameras. We have to figure out what kind of message the killer is trying to send if we are going to stop him."

Dr. Applewhite was frowning down at the images, and she placed them beside Zoe's notes to run through the calculations Zoe had already made.

"Your working seems sound," she said, after a while had passed. "I can't see anywhere else to take it that you haven't already gone. This is extremely advanced—beyond even the level that I work at."

Zoe's heart sunk in her chest. She had been sure, so sure, that Dr. Applewhite would have the answers. Now, it seemed, those hopes were dashed.

She was already thinking through alternatives, trying to figure out what she was going to say to Shelley, when Dr. Applewhite spoke up again.

"I know some people who might be able to help," she said. "Professors. A couple of mathematicians who work in other fields. If I can show this to them, I might be able to get a bit further with it. This is the kind of challenge that they will all love, so at least we're bound to get some skilled hands on deck."

Zoe nodded her approval. "That would be helpful."

Dr. Applewhite tucked her graying bob behind one ear and looked up, fixing Zoe with that same curious stare now. "How are you holding up on this one? It's not often a math question comes up that has you stumped."

Zoe considered lying for a brief moment, but then let her shoulders slump. "A little like a failure. This is my specialty. I should at least be able to work it out. If I cannot, who in the FBI is going to?"

In anyone else's voice, it would have sounded like a brag. To Zoe, it was pure fact. Analysts and their like might spend all day working with numbers, but they didn't have the instinctive grasp on them that she did. They couldn't look at an equation on the page and see the answer as clearly as if it was written out beside it. At least, that was the case for her usually.

This one was something else.

"You can't be expected to solve everything. No FBI agent in the history of the Bureau ever had a one hundred percent solve rate."

Zoe smiled a wan smile. "I am sure that there have been examples. Agents who were killed or retired just after solving their first case, for example."

Dr. Applewhite rolled her eyes. "Trust you to find the loophole. All right, I will make some calls and get these equations out in front of some of my colleagues. I won't tell them what it's for—just that it's urgent and a big challenge. That should intrigue them enough to get them working on it. I will let you know the moment anyone makes a breakthrough."

"Or anything else, too," Zoe prompted. "If someone finds a mistake, or a sign that something is missing. We were not able to fully check the first body to see if anything was missed by the photographer. Bear in mind that we also do not know whether this is intended to be one equation or two separate problems."

"Understood." Dr. Applewhite placed the photographs down on the desk in front of her, two inches off to the right, closer to her laptop. A gesture that reassured Zoe of her intention to begin work as soon as she had the chance. "Now, what about Dr. Monk's recommendations? Have you thought anymore about—"

Zoe's ringtone blasted out from her pocket, accompanied by strong buzzing. Saved by the bell, she thought, as she made an apologetic face and answered the call.

"Special Agent Prime."

"Z, it's me. I got a hit in the professor's emails."

"I am on my way," Zoe told her, ending the call and jumping out of her seat with a nod to her mentor. Whatever it was, it had to be more promising than the nothing that they had.

Chapter Seven

Zoe pulled the car into the campus parking lot. At this time of night, the evening drawing down rapidly, it was fairly full—the cars belonging to students who lived in the various dorms and apartments scattered around. Each of them bore a university permit stuck to their front windshield. Zoe's car had something better—an FBI sticker.

"Read it to me again?" Zoe asked. She was still unsure about Shelley's theory. Being angry about a dropped grade was one thing, but angry enough to kill?

Shelley brought up the email on her phone without even a sigh of frustration, to her credit. She had saved the screenshot and brought it along as proof—proof they would need if they were going to confront the student who had sent it.

"'Professor,'" she read. "'I can't believe you flunked me. Like, are you serious? I tried really goddamn hard on his paper and you just decided to kick me off the course! Teachers are supposed to help and support. Thanks a whole fucking bunch. You're the worst professor I ever had. I hope you get fired. I'm not the only one who hates your guts. You're going to get hauled over the coals if the dean listens to our complaints. Try sleeping well tonight, asshole.'"

Zoe had already zoned out by the time Shelley was done. She had heard it a couple of times before, and this time had not changed her opinion. It was student bluster, that was all. Threats made to his career, not to his life.

Not to mention that the student in question was studying English, not math. It was not a close enough connection. How could this barely literate student have known to write out complex equations? Complex enough to stump experts?

And besides, even if this kid was angry with the professor, it didn't at all explain why he would have gone after the first victim—the student.

"Well?" Shelley prompted.

Zoe realized that she had been sitting in silence, failing to respond to Shelley's reading. She shrugged her shoulders now. "It sounds like nothing."

"Come on, he's directly threatening the professor, Z," Shelley said. "And this allusion to other disgruntled students—what if he knows others who might have done it? At the very least, we need to bring him in for questioning."

Zoe stared out across the dark campus, her arms folded across her chest in front of the steering wheel. "If you say so."

It clearly was not the answer that Shelley had been hoping for, as she made an annoyed sound in the back of her throat and turned away.

Her phone buzzed at almost precisely the same moment, and she looked down to read the incoming message. "I've just had an email from a secretary in the admissions department. She sent over Jones's schedule."

"Jones?" Zoe interrupted.

This time, Shelley did sigh and roll her eyes. "Jensen Jones, the student we're here to see. I know you don't think it's much of a lead, but I thought you were at least paying attention."

Zoe shrugged again, offering no apology. She had better, more important things to focus on. The equations. The fact that she still wasn't any closer to solving them. Waiting around for Dr. Applewhite's contacts to look at them and get back to her was like agony.

"Anyway, this is important. Jones was also taking a physics class. And guess who happened to be the student instructor for that class?"

Zoe stared back at her, unflinching. She wasn't about to play this game.

Shelley pushed on, undeterred. "Cole Davidson. As in, victim number one. Jones has a personal connection to both of the victims."

"But he does not take math." Zoe couldn't hold it back any longer. She refused to believe that there was any way the equations were random, just scrawling meant to distract them. They had a key part to play in this case. They had to.

Because if they didn't, then Zoe wasn't as useful to this case as she thought she was, and it was all just a boring, run of the mill murder. Why it bothered her so much that that might be the case, she couldn't fully say. All she knew was that she needed to solve the equations, and for them to be the key.

"Look, I know you could pull rank if you wanted to. You're the senior agent. But I don't want to end up with an unsolved case and not be able to say that we left no stone unturned. I'm going in to question him," Shelley said decisively, opening her door and getting out of the car.

Zoe sat for a moment, then sighed and opened her own door. At the end of the day, they were partners. They worked together. Even if Zoe had no belief at all that this was a viable need, she was still supposed to support her partner.

So, she would.

She caught up with Shelley, who was striding as fast as her legs could take her across the campus, some minutes later. There was a crackling energy coming from the other woman, an anger that bristled from her like the spines on a porcupine. Zoe was familiar with that kind of sensation. She was always provoking anger in others, often at times when she couldn't work out what she had done wrong.

At least this time, she knew.

"I will take your lead," Zoe said. "If you feel that this kid will give us something, I will back you up."

Shelley's steps faltered a little, before she resumed her course. "Thank you," she said, a little too primly. Zoe gathered that she was still upset, but why? She had given Shelley what she wanted, hadn't she?

Such questions would have to be left for later, or preferably never at all, because they had arrived outside an apartment building just off the side of the campus. Shelley had closed the map application on her phone, by which Zoe understood that they must have arrived. She also knew just standing there in the street that the music booming out of the windows, even though they were closed, was above city regulations for the volume of noise audible in public at night.

A college student, looking to be nineteen years old at most, was stumbling out of the doorway as they approached. He had a red cup in his hand, and his hands were fumbling with a cigarette. When he looked up and saw the two women coming toward him, his eyes widened to almost a comical degree. The one fluid ounce of liquid in the cup was thrown over his shoulder to land on some bushes, and he walked away quickly, clutching the now-empty plastic receptacle as if his life depended on keeping it out of their hands.

"Party," Zoe said, recognizing enough of the signs.

Zoe pulled her phone out again and brought up a photograph of Jensen Jones from his college registration. He was young, fairly clean-cut. Brown hair, a wide nose, brown eyes. Nothing at all special.

Which was bad news, because of what Shelley said next. "We'll have to keep an eye out for him. I guess most of them will scatter and run as soon as we get there. We kind of obviously look like FBI, or at least cops. Might have to catch him as he tries to get away."

"Having a party right after murdering two people?" Zoe asked. "Is that really considered a normal reaction?"

"Not normal, no, but it has happened," Shelley said. "I could cite a couple of cases, but it's probably more efficient for us to grab him and find out for sure."

"After you," Zoe suggested, gesturing toward the door.

Shelley drew a deep breath as if she were steeling herself, then nodded. "Let's go."

Beyond the door of the apartment building, the noise was much louder. To complicate their search, there were three open doors on the ground floor alone—the residents of each of the apartments opening their own spaces up to be a new area of the party. It had spilled across the corridor, up the stairs, and—judging at least by the sheer number of teenagers moving in all directions—through every apartment in the building.

The appearance of Zoe and Shelley was not immediately noted. A couple of students saw them and ducked past them out the door, no doubt wanting to get themselves as far away from trouble as possible.

But then the worst possible thing happened: one of the kids, a jock standing at six feet with the build of a quarterback, yelled out in panic. "The cops are here!"

The call went through the building like wildfire, and panic started to set in. There was no use in trying to stay incognito. Zoe reached into her inner jacket pocket for her badge and brandished it in the air. "FBI. This party is breaking up. Now!"

The effect was immediate and palpable. Thirty students ran past her in quick succession, all of them from down in the lower apartment rooms. The word was spreading up the stairs, too, and people were clattering down, sloshing their beers onto the carpet as they tripped and stumbled.

Zoe waited in the downstairs lobby while Shelley went into all three of the ground floor rooms in turn, scattering more students out through them as she did so. Even from where she stood, making no attempt to catch any of the students who continued to run by her, Zoe could see that the place was a mess. Crumpled red cups, spilled food and drink, and no doubt the occasional patch of vomit covered every surface in sight. It had been a big one—the legendary kind of party that kids talk about for months. Too bad they had ended it.

Zoe couldn't say she felt any kind of misplaced nostalgia for them. She had rarely been invited to parties of any kind, and it was even rarer that she attended them. Then, as now, this kind of party was too overwhelming. The noise, the people in all directions, the intoxication and temptation of forbidden alcohol—and, judging by the smells in the air, other substances, too.

With the benefit of extra years of experience, it was still all Zoe could do to concentrate on studying the faces of those who ran by her. She checked each of them for the youth in the photograph, but although there were plenty of near matches, none of them were the real Jensen Jones. She felt like a stone in the middle of a river, the current washing around her. There were plenty of interesting things that caught her eye, angles and figures and signs, but they went by so quickly that she was barely even able to register them before they were gone.

Shelley reemerged from the third room, shaking her head. Zoe tore her eyes back toward the stairs, just in time to see someone charging down them. A young woman wearing a collection of twelve bottle tops all strung together around her neck, clattering against one another as she ran—

"There!" Shelley shouted.

Zoe pulled her attention back from the girl too late, seeing only another blur passing by her. By the way Shelley was pointing, Zoe knew that it must have been their guy. She swore under her breath—he was through the door already.

She twisted on her feet and sprang after him, keeping him in her sights as he raced away. He was five foot ten, built athletically, muscles straining easily in his calves as his arms pumped up and down. Young, in shape, and clearly an experienced runner.

Zoe had barely gone five steps before she knew she didn't have a hope in hell of catching him.

In her head, the campus spread out before her like a map, topography and angles of incline included. He was snaking away toward the left, making for a group of small buildings that dotted the edge of the campus. Behind them was a fence, built to maintain a barrier between the college and the surrounding town.

Zoe thought faster than she could run. His path would necessarily have to be curved, following the line of the fence, before he reached a gap and a gate for pedestrians to pass through. That was if he had even brought his student ID with him, which she knew already was needed for exiting at that point, right next to several college facilities.

"Keep on him!" she yelled over her shoulder, seeing Shelley from the corner of her eye as she herself peeled away to the right. At this speed, he would always outrun her. But she could cross a shorter distance in the same time, and calculating his miles per hour against hers, she knew that she could meet him at the gate.

But only if she cut a straight line across an open quad, through a narrow corridor between two buildings, and then directly across the parking lot behind it.

Only if someone didn't get in her way.

Zoe pumped her arms and legs harder, speeding up even when she thought she was at her limit, straining against the cold night air streaming into her lungs. It was not often, these days, that she had a real athletic challenge to cope with. And she wasn't as young as he was. But she pushed, intending to make damn sure that she would be there in time—even if there was a stumbling block in her way.

The quad passed by in a blur, then it was a shot through the corridor, the thin gap thankfully empty of any other bodies to stumble into her path. The ground underfoot changed to the harsh, jarring feel of tarmac, punishing her feet for choosing to be clothed in plain dress shoes instead of trainers.

Zoe could still not see the fence on the other side of the buildings, but she could see the gate. She rushed forward with another surge of adrenaline. If she didn't get there in time…

Chapter Eight

There was no time to lose. Zoe gave a final, hard push, forcing her body beyond its natural breaking point.

Zoe's heart pounded in time with her feet across the parking lot, and she crashed to a halt as her body collided with another. She thrust out her arms instinctively to keep hold of him, and pushed Jensen Jones up against the ten-foot fence so that he could not use his superior build to get away.

Shelley was only a few moments behind. She was heavily out of breath and red in the face with strands of hair flying out of her chignon, but she was there. She assisted Zoe in slapping a pair of handcuffs around his wrists, behind his back, as they panted out warnings about running from law enforcement and the right to question him. He only hung his head, trying to catch his own breath as well.

Zoe's whole body felt like it had woken up. Air and light had supplanted the spaces in between her joints, the stretching out of long-dormant muscles feeling wonderful. Of course, there was also pain; particularly in her ankles, which had not at all enjoyed the jolting across the parking lot. Overall, she felt great. There was something about the rush of wind in your hair as you raced someone else—and won.

The apartment building felt different to Zoe, now that it was empty of everyone except for herself, Shelley, and Jensen. The guests had scattered to the four winds, and the residents along with them. No doubt they were going for plausible deniability.

Zoe poked around the apartment that housed Jensen Jones, sniffing at thirteen cups still full of a liquid that was definitely not water and checking four ashtrays. Shelley had sat the kid down on the sofa in the open-plan room, dragging a dining chair over to sit opposite him. There were not many clean seating options left, so Zoe opted to stand and wander.

Despite his apparent inebriation, the kid was not far gone enough to misunderstand what was happening to him. In fact, he appeared to have sobered up quite nicely with the joint impact of his run and the revelation that they were FBI, not local cops.

"It was just a party," he muttered, his eyes sweeping the floor as if looking for a traitor sign of something more serious. "Since when does the FBI get called to parties?"

"We don't, Mr. Jones," Shelley said, with an air of conspiracy. "Actually, we were looking for you specifically. In connection with another matter."

Zoe was already up to twenty-two cups. Just how many people had been squeezed into this party? Given that they were still running when Zoe and Shelley left the building, she had to guess at more than a hundred.

There was nothing but confusion on Jones's face. "What other matter?" he asked.

"There was a professor who tragically lost his life here yesterday," Shelley said. Zoe watched her face, watching her watch him for a sign. She was getting to know Shelley better. It was easier for her to read Shelley than a stranger. "Professor Henderson was your former professor, was he not?"

"Yeah," Jones said, then sat up straighter with a look of alarm. "Hey, but listen, I wasn't involved in all that!"

"How did you feel about Professor Henderson?" Shelley pressed.

"Uh, he was okay. I mean. It's super sad that he died. Everyone's in shock."

There were seven stubs of cigarettes in the ashtrays. They looked hand-rolled. Probably not tobacco. Zoe lowered her nose slightly and sniffed, her suspicion confirmed by the scent coming off them. And in Jones's apartment, too. He wasn't going to be able to put up much of an argument that it wasn't him, or that he didn't know the party was going on.

"I'd like to read you something," Shelley said, taking out her phone. "Let's see . . . it starts like this: 'Professor, I can't believe you flunked me. Like, are you serious? I tried really goddamn hard on his paper and you just decided to kick me off the course!'"

"Okay, okay." Jones held his hands up. He obviously recognized his own words. "Yes, I sent it. But it—it doesn't mean I did anything! I was just super angry when he flunked me. After I sent the email I felt kinda bad. I should have been nicer. Maybe he would've let me back into class."

"So you're saying that you sent this angry, threatening email to Professor Henderson, coincidentally right before he was brutally murdered in a manner that smacks of personal anger, but you have nothing to do with that?"

Jones swallowed and looked down. "I get how it looks. I do. But I wasn't *that* angry. I'll just take a different course next semester. Try something different. I haven't decided my major yet anyway."

Shelley switched tacks with a cool and effortless manner, something that Zoe was beginning more and more to admire. "Cole Davidson was the SI in your physics class, wasn't he?"

Jones blinked: once, then twice. "I…yes, I guess he was. I mean, I never really spoke to him all that much."

"You attended class, did you not?"

"Yes, but, I, I mean, I didn't *know* him or anything, I—I mean—are you really suggesting that I…?"

"You tell us, Mr. Jones. Did you have anything to do with this? Or do you know who did?"

Jones shook his head five times in long sweeps side to side, his mouth working soundlessly as the reality of his situation washed over him. Zoe counted beads of sweat on his forehead. He was nervous, but it was hard to tell if that was because he had been caught or because he was being falsely accused.

"No, wait, this isn't right," he said, at last. "I wasn't—when Cole went missing. I wasn't in that area. I had class—a night class—you can check the records. And when the professor was killed last night—it was in the night, wasn't it?"

"Around eleven p.m.," Zoe spoke up, examining a sideboard behind him. He flinched at the sound of her voice.

"Right, so, then, I couldn't have done that either," Jones babbled, holding his hands in front of him in a gesture of appeal. "I was working. I work in a bar. Extra money, to get me through college. My boss will tell you. And I'll be on the cameras there, too."

There was a moment of silence that met this proclamation. Zoe and Shelley met eyes, both thinking the same thing. He had an alibi, one that would be exceptionally easy to check. And they would check it—of course they would. But for now, he was looking increasingly unlikely as a suspect, and they would have to let him go.

Or, at least, let him go to a different kind of law enforcement.

"You're twenty years old, isn't that right, Mr. Jones?" Shelley asked.

He nodded mutely.

"Well, I can smell the alcohol on your breath from here. Special Agent Prime?"

"There are smoked joints in the ashtray."

"That's two counts." Shelley smiled, as if she and Jones were sharing a friendly discussion. "Not your best week for decisions, is it?"

Jones groaned. "Oh, come on, I didn't do anything. You can let it go just this once, right?"

"Wrong." Zoe loomed behind him. "We will wait here with you until the local police can come and pick you up. We would not want you to go and dispose of any evidence."

Jones buried his head in his hands as Shelley got up to make the call, and Zoe watched him carefully for signs of running again. The tension in his muscles remained slack, and the angle of his feet to the floor remained the same; he was not priming to leap.

Even the satisfaction of knowing that she had been right was not enough to make her feel better. There was still the not at all small matter of two murders to solve, and this night had not taken them any closer to doing that. If anything, it had put them further away.

Zoe checked her watch. Twenty-four hours since Professor Henderson had been murdered. They only had another twenty-four to really get it right.

Beyond that, their chances of solving this case dropped dramatically, and there was a murder-crazed mathematician out there who would get away with it.

Chapter Nine

Back at the FBI field office, Zoe felt like tearing her hair out. That would at least allow her to feel something other than this screaming frustration, the numbers seeming to dance on the page and taunt her the more she looked at them.

She had copied both equations onto large sheets of paper and tacked them to the walls, but it made no difference. She could still only get two-thirds of the way through the workings before she became hopelessly, utterly lost.

It was as if the last part of the equation just made no sense at all. It was so far above her head that it might as well have been written in a foreign alphabet.

"It's late," Shelley sighed.

She was right; it was. After waiting for the local cops to show up and handing Jensen Jones into their custody, then making their way back to HQ before settling in to work the slim leads they had, it was now past midnight. Pythagoras and Euler would be hungry, and Shelley's daughter was no doubt already in bed since hours ago. They should have both been at home.

If this had been a normal, paperwork or testifying in court kind of day, they might have been. But this was a murder investigation kind of day, and that meant the work didn't stop until someone was behind bars—or put into the morgue before they could take another life.

"You should go home." Zoe nodded. She felt a little guilty, Shelley being away from home like this. A pair of grumpy cats were very much used to their owner not being home every day, and they had auto-feeders she could turn on whenever she was out of town for this very purpose. A small child would not understand why her mother was always late.

"You, too," Shelley said. She had picked up her bag and coat, but stood in front of Zoe now without moving. Zoe caught the message loud and clear: Shelley wouldn't go until she agreed to do so, as well.

She sighed and started to gather her things.

"Are you going to be okay?" Shelley asked. "You look tired. You'll be fine for the drive home?"

"I am about as tired as you are," Zoe pointed out. "I just want to crack this equation. Get somewhere with the case."

"We are getting somewhere. There's only so much we can do when we're running low on sleep. A good night's rest, and who knows? You might see something new when you approach it with fresh eyes."

If Zoe had wanted advice from schoolroom posters, she could have looked it up herself. She shook her head brusquely, and did not reply.

"Seriously, Z. Take some time for yourself. If you don't look after yourself, you won't be any help to anyone. We need you sharp on this one," Shelley said, obviously not reading Zoe's irritation.

"I understand the importance of sleep," Zoe snapped. "I do not intend to sit up until morning studying the equations. You do not have to worry."

Shelley paused at the door, looking back at her with a softly trouble expression, a frown that only slightly creased her forehead. "I do worry, though. I see how hard you are on yourself."

Not that Zoe had ever had that kind of mother—but Shelley sure as hell sounded like the stereotypical mother figure she had seen on TV. All nag, as if Zoe was just a child. Never mind that she was senior in her role, she was senior in age, too. She did not need a mother figure, and if she did, she wouldn't choose a younger woman who was supposed to be taking her orders.

"I will be fine," she said, her tone short and clipped, and brushed past Shelley to move quickly down the corridor. She opted to take the stairs, knowing Shelley would go down in the elevator, so that they did not have to share one another's company all the way to the parking lot. The elevator moved at a much faster rate per floor than Zoe could manage on foot, particularly given the twists and turns of the stairwell, but she took them at a slow walking pace just to be sure.

As she walked down the fifteen steps in each block, and counted off the blocks before she would be underground with her car, Zoe's mind was still on the equations. For all that she had said to Shelley, she probably wouldn't be able to sleep well with the unsolvable numbers whirling around and around in her head.

They dominated her mind all through the drive home. Maybe Shelley had a little bit of a point about the state of mental distraction she was in, but she wasn't about to admit that anytime soon. The equations just didn't seem to make sense.

Whatever happened tomorrow, Zoe could only hope that she would hear something from one of Dr. Applewhite's colleagues. They needed a break. No, she needed a break. Zoe desperately needed to know the answer to these puzzles—before they drove her mad.

As Zoe lay awake, staring up at her dark ceiling and listening to the soothing rainforest sounds that she played at night to shut out the calculations, a different scene entirely came into her head. Instead of the numbers, she thought about Dr. Applewhite. About a time, long ago, when she had been a young woman—and just beginning to trust Dr. Applewhite more than she had trusted anyone. Maybe more than she had ever even trusted herself.

She had been so young back then. So young it was almost painful to think of it now. Like all people of that age, she had thought she was so mature. After being emancipated from her parents and striking out on her own, Zoe had felt like there was nothing she could not do. She was strong, independent, fierce.

And on the other side of the coin, utterly vulnerable and alone.

No one knew, back then, what she could do. There had never been anyone she had felt she could trust enough. Throughout her whole childhood and her early teenage years, Zoe's mother had pounded the message into her brain: *Don't tell anyone. Keep quiet. Don't let them notice.*

It was her mother's claim that Zoe's skills came from the devil that had tortured her the most. Always, whenever she thought about living life more openly, it came back to that. The fear of rejection, of social isolation, of people looking at her like she was evil.

Zoe never wanted to go through that ever again.

Part of the reason she pushed people away, held them at a distance, was that fear. Maybe they looked at her like she was a bitch now, so stuck-up and aloof that they couldn't stand her. But they didn't know the truth, and so she would take the alternative.

That fear had almost swallowed her voice and left her mute when she decided to come clean with Dr. Applewhite. But alongside it was another fear, one that had been steadily growing ever since she had first left home: the fear that she would never find a place to belong. She wanted reassurance, wanted someone who would understand. With just one person, she thought, she would be able to go on.

So it was that she decided to spill it all, to pour her heart out in front of Dr. Applewhite and wait to see if she would stomp on it. Maybe it had not been that melodramatic from the outside; just a young girl coming out with the truth, despite the bad experiences she had had in the past. But for Zoe, it had been one of the worst moments of her life, waiting for Dr. Applewhite to respond.

Her response, when it came, had become one of the best moments of Zoe's life, just an instant later.

"I can see numbers," Zoe said, her words rushing over one another, almost becoming garbled in her desire to finally get them out. "Everywhere, in everything. Calculations and angles. Counts. They are just there when I look."

"Tell me everything," Dr. Applewhite said, her eyes lighting up with fascination.

Zoe hesitated, looking up in surprise. Could it really be that someone was interested in her ability—in a positive way?

"Zoe, what you are describing to me is a very special gift. Tell me how it works. What can you see now?" Dr. Applewhite asked.

There was still doubt, but Zoe pushed on, did as she was told. "Your hair is just under eight inches long. Seven point eight inches, I think. You weigh one hundred and twenty-two pounds and you are five feet, six inches tall. There are fifteen individual pieces of wood in the floorboards of this room. The fingernail of the ring finger on your left hand is four millimeters longer than the one on your right hand. Your—"

Zoe cut herself off, realizing that Dr. Applewhite was staring at her with an expression that Zoe did not know how to read. Had she said something wrong?

Did Dr. Applewhite think she was evil, like her own mother always had? Was she about to throw her out of the office?

"That is absolutely remarkable," Dr. Applewhite said instead, leaning over the table and squeezing Zoe's hand. "Thank you so much for sharing this with me."

And that had been the most relieving, most incredible, moment of Zoe's life. A weight lifted from her shoulders. A light turned on in front of her eyes.

She wasn't evil. She wasn't even bad.

Maybe, just maybe, there was a chance that she could be amazing.

Dr. Applewhite had never judged, never thought badly of Zoe for the things she could do. Instead, she had praised her, been amazed at her skills. She had always wanted to know more. Not because Zoe was a test subject—her study of synesthesia had come after they met, not before—but because she could do something that normal people could not do.

Dr. Applewhite had called it a superpower, not a curse.

From then on, Zoe had had the one thing she had always wanted. Support. Someone to lean on. Someone she could fully and honestly be herself around. Dr. Applewhite never reacted with shock or revulsion when Zoe could tell her the precise angle of a chair leg and how much it needed to be adjusted by to be fixed, or weigh her with her eyes.

She had fully embraced Zoe and all that she could do, for who she honestly was. Finally, Zoe had found someone in whom her trust was not misplaced.

And now there was Shelley.

Telling Shelley her secret had been easier, much easier than the first time. Zoe had the advantage of years of life experience, and years of support from someone who did not turn away. She also had the pressure of her job, of a case that needed to be solved in order to save lives. Though the trepidation had been there, Zoe had been able to push past it and tell Shelley the truth.

Like Dr. Applewhite before her, Shelley had been open and accepting. Had called it a gift.

Back then, Zoe had been happy that she had decided to come clean. She had felt that it improved their relationship, made it easier for Zoe to do her job. But now?

The doubts were creeping in. For all the acceptance that Shelley had shown, she was not as careful with the truth as Zoe had asked her to be. Telling the Special Agent in Charge that she was "good with math" was too close for comfort. Now the nagging, the difference in opinion about how the job should be done, chasing down pointless leads instead of trusting Zoe's focus.

Dr. Applewhite had been a supportive face, but also a kindred spirit. She believed in the cause the same way that Zoe did. Saving lives, helping people, fighting injustice—that was what Dr. Applewhite did all day long in her continued studies of conditions like Zoe's own. She understood how important it was that Zoe's secret never became knowledge amongst her superiors.

Shelley did not share that understanding. Which made Zoe wonder what else she did not share. What else separated them, alongside the few things that they had in common? They were apart in age, in family status, even in their approach to people. What if telling Shelley her darkest secret had been a mistake?

In the end, it was that thought, not the equations, that kept Zoe up all night. Without the FBI, she had nothing. No purpose to her life. What if telling Shelley about the numbers was the thing that was ultimately going to end her career—and take away her reason for being?

Chapter Ten

He was waiting in the parking lot at the hospital, waiting for it to slowly empty out.

The doctor would come out soon. He needed to see the doctor. Needed to make the doctor pay.

He drummed his fingers on the steering wheel of his refuge. His hiding place. Like a hunter. Waiting for a deer to come along that he could shoot.

Not a deer. Too cute, too nice. Something savage and wild.

He would eat the—deer for dinner.

Deer, deer . . . what was . . . what was he thinking about?

The doctor.

His eyes were trained on the exit, the entrance, the window, the—what do you call it? He waited for a familiar sight. Someone that he recognized. A refuge that he had seen before, because he looked it up, looked it up on purpose.

No, not just anyone. The doctor had to pay. He was going to smash the doctor's head in like he did the others. The blood and brains spilling out over his fingers like—snakes. Like? The snakes out like brains over blood fingers. Like that. Yes, like that.

He cut himself off with a memory, a gasp of fear still that always came when he thought about it. The cr—the bad thing. The thing that had ruined everything, that flooded into his mind with such clarity he wanted to wail for it to stop.

He didn't know how he got there. There was nothing in his memory, a gap between getting into the car and then here. Now he was afraid, knowing instinctively that something was wrong. Something had happened.

The car was still around him but not quite quiet. Small noises, like dripping and the settling of metal. He heard those first. Then he pried his eyes open—and why were they closed?—to a light that startled him with its intensity. He gasped and shut his eyes again, wanting to shut it out.

But he had to know. He forced himself to endure the pain of the brightness, his eyes starting to adjust the longer he held them open. Good. Now he could focus a little more, look around. Like he suspected, he was still in the car.

But the car was . . . well, no longer the car.

On the passenger side, right next to him, everything was mangled metal and twisted and ripped fabric. The seat was destroyed, the frame of the window almost reaching out as if it would touch his elbow. There was something in the car—actually in *the car, so close he could touch it—a kind of concrete structure, a block that extended upward.*

He followed it up with his eyes and found the source of the startling light. A streetlight.

He had crashed into a streetlight.

The realization flooded in, and in the next moment, the fact that his side of the car was undamaged. The steering wheel was still in place, the door unbent, nothing at all out of order. He had escaped what might have been a very nasty death indeed.

He laughed in relief, but the movement sent pain ricocheting through his head in a way he had never known. He groaned and put his hands up to his temples, grasping there. Something wet—something slick. He pulled his hands down and looked, and saw that his fingers were red with blood.

His eyes focused a little beyond, in front of the steering wheel. There was blood there, too. He had hit his head.

There was the sound of a siren in the distance, and as he looked ahead, he caught a glimpse of himself in the reflection from a piece of glass that stubbornly hung on to the bent and twisted structure of the windshield frame. Wide eyes under a forehead smeared with blood, pooling down it. It dripped down, over his left eye and onto his cheek.

The siren was getting closer, as he looked at himself in horror.

Maybe he had not escaped something nasty at all.

The doctor!

He sprang forward, his hands on the handle of the—window. He would get out and go toward him, distract him, get him alone. But—wait!

Over there—the man—another colleague. A robe like all doctors wore, white around his shoulders. The doctor, the doctor! The doctor had to pay! Pay for this agony, this jumble, this mess!

No, no, no, no, no—the other man was ruining everything. Everything. He walked with the doctor and talked with him, flapping his—arm as the words came out, talking and talking and just never shutting up. The doctor talked back and they walked and they talked out into the parking lot.

He shrank in the seat and watched, watched them, waited for something. The third one. The third brains like snakes, it had to be. The sky formed—ribbons like murky water to fall above him, falling, falling. The doctor was getting wet. He went back to the hospital. The other man ran the distance to his refuge and got in and slammed the window shut behind him.

That man, that man! Blast that man and damned him and let him rot in—in space! He ruined it all! The man's engine started, the light was on through the window, the thrum-thrum of the car moved away. The sky ribbons fell and fell like tears from above, like the whole sky could feel how he was feeling.

And who could know how he was feeling? All of it gone, lost, vanished on the wind like smoke from a—cannon. Disappeared and gone. His mind, his brilliant, beautiful mind. It was everything.

Now the snakes were crawling around up there and the doctor was on call all night and the lights were going on around him and the people ran under ribbons falling so fast. The window mist was the fog in his head, the pain, the words falling like snakes and ribbons.

He covered his eyes until the headache subsided and drove away, back home, back to wait for another chance. He had to make the doctor pay.

Chapter Eleven

Zoe was already wide awake, dressed and ready to go, when her alarm went off in the morning. It had been a restless night, and almost a sleepless one. She had tormented herself all night long, before rising sleep-deprived and groggy to admit defeat.

Even if sleep eluded her, she was determined that the answer to the equations would not. She had some of the finest minds in the math world on the case; even if she was not good enough to figure them out herself, someone else would. That was the mantra she soothed herself with as she drove to the field office, sipping hot coffee and only just managing to concentrate on the road.

She had barely stepped two feet into the office when her cell rang.

"Zoe," Dr. Applewhite exclaimed breathlessly down the phone.

Zoe was instantly on alert, her body tensing. "Have you discovered something?" she asked.

"No. Well, yes." Dr. Applewhite hesitated. Zoe got the impression of movement from the noise in the background of the call: rustling papers and fabrics, footsteps pacing, the unusual cadence of Dr. Applewhite's voice. She was pacing backward and forward. "I've heard back from most of the contacts I reached out to. You know what mathematicians are like; can't resist a challenge. Most of them had a bit of a sleepless night."

Zoe refrained from admitting that she had had the same experience. The less small talk the better; she wanted the answer, and she wanted it now. "Go on."

"Well, here's the thing. They, almost all of them, said the same thing. All agreed they couldn't solve it—couldn't make any real headway. But these are some of the best minds in the world, Zoe—really, the sharpest. If they can't solve it . . . anyway, they tell me the equations are impossible. A few of them even asked me if it was possible that a practical joke had been played on me. Because, you see—what they think is—the equations are *wrong*."

There was a beat. Zoe retraced the conversation mentally, Dr. Applewhite's last word hanging in her ears. Had she really heard it correctly? "Wrong?"

"Precisely. Whoever wrote them down—well, they're either writing gibberish, or they don't understand what they're writing. Several parts of it are just garbled, just absolute nonsense. There's no wonder you couldn't get anywhere with it. No one can."

Zoe started pacing up and down, mirroring the frantic actions of her mentor, who was clearly just as excited about all of this as Zoe herself. Except that now something was wrong, something heavy sitting inside her chest and threatening to choke her. *Wrong?* Could that really be the case?

"I do not understand," Zoe admitted, glancing up as the door opened to admit Shelley.

"I just don't think your killer even knows what they're writing on the bodies. This really widens things up, don't you think? Realistically, if they're so hard that not even our best and brightest can solve them, you would be looking for the best mathematician in the world. The odds of that happening are very low, you must admit."

"Astronomically low," Zoe muttered in reply, closing her eyes briefly against the deluge of calculations that instantly appeared in her mind, zeroes spiraling off into the distance.

Shelley was giving her a questioning frown as she settled her handbag down on a chair and removed her jacket, watching her carefully. Zoe turned away so that she didn't have to meet her gaze. There was too much to explain, and unlike others who could seemingly multitask, Zoe had never been good at carrying on two conversations at once.

"It seems the most logical explanation would be that this person is simply, well, damaged. Psychologically speaking. A schizophrenic with paranoid delusions, or so forth. Perhaps they think they are writing down something of great importance. Maybe they believe it is a message from God, even. The point is, they have some kind of mental problem. There's no math in it at all."

That heavy stone of disappointment had settled firmly in Zoe's stomach. It didn't feel right. None of it felt right. But how much of that was her own desire to be right about the importance of the writing? She couldn't be sure. "Right," she said, hearing her own voice distantly. "I will take that into account as we investigate further."

There was a pause on the other end, before Dr. Applewhite spoke again, softer and soothingly. "Zoe, I know it must be difficult to take in. I understand that you wanted the equations to mean something. The thing is, they simply don't."

"I hear you," Zoe said. It was the only truth she could offer just then. "Thank you for going to all of this trouble for me."

Dr. Applewhite was making overtures of kindness, suggesting that she would do anything Zoe needed, but Zoe had already begun to tune her out. She was looking at the blown-up photographs of the equations, printed in a scrawling hand across the torsos of two dead men.

"I will talk to you again soon," she said, hanging up the call. She did not have enough presence of mind to know whether Dr. Applewhite had been in mid-sentence when she interrupted.

"Is it bad news?" Shelley asked, quietly.

Zoe had almost forgotten she was in the room. "My contact, for the math professors. They do not feel that there is any lead in the equations. Apparently, they are impossible to solve. The word used was 'gibberish.'"

Shelley took a breath, blew out a whistle. "Wow. Are we sure about that?"

Zoe searched within herself, trying to find the answer. Did she really believe it? "I do not know," she said, at last. "It does not feel right. I thought these equations were the key to solving it all. I—I still do. How can they be meaningless?"

Shelley circled their desks to stand next to Zoe, looking down at the pictures. She patted Zoe's hand lightly, then tapped one of the images. "They aren't meaningless. Not to us. Even if the equations have no solution, these were written by our perpetrator. That means they have a lot of clues for us. State of mind, handwriting, even the pen he used. That's forensic evidence. We can still use these to put him behind bars."

"Or her," Zoe said automatically, though it was true that the physical evidence suggested the strength of a male. Still, she had been caught out by that once in the past. A woman who had trained as a wrestler, the musculature on her arms far above that of the average female—or male, for that matter. Her strength had been enough to snuff out a life without need for any tools other than her own body.

"All hope is not lost, is what I'm saying."

Zoe continued to stare down at the images. If Dr. Applewhite was right, Zoe had just wasted some of the most crucial hours of the case fixating on something that meant nothing. And she had been *so sure.* Could this really be meaningless? Really?

"You aren't the only one who had trouble sleeping," Shelley said, giving Zoe a sympathetic smile. Zoe briefly wondered how Shelley could tell, but then, she hadn't looked in a mirror that morning. The bags under her eyes were probably deeper and darker than ever. "I spent a few hours searching online. Take a look at these."

She had a sheath of papers that she was distributing across the desk, covering over the crime scene photographs. Zoe wanted to protest, but she held herself back. She would sound petty. Like she couldn't let the equation theory go.

She didn't want to let it go, but that was beside the point. When people wanted her to forget something, and she didn't, there were often arguments and interventions set to follow. Zoe didn't want that. She could at least pretend she was getting over it, in front of others.

"These two are from local papers, and those are from scientific journals," Shelley was explaining, pointing at the various printouts. Each of them bore a photograph of the same man, some from different angles; the headlines were all inflammatory. "See here? *Professor loses post over controversy.* It sounds like this guy got into a pretty public showdown. He was a fairly well-respected theoretical physicist, until he got into an argument with another professor. Things escalated, words turned to blows. The police intervened, and it turns out our guy was drunk on the job. He lost his position, and his reputation hit the rocks. Students and colleagues started coming out of the woodwork, accusing him of inappropriate conduct because of his alcoholism."

"And he was teaching here?" Zoe asked, nodding as she followed the story. It was a convincing picture. A man with an ax to grind.

"Yes. And here's the best part." Shelley paused, flashing Zoe a smile. "Guess who the other professor was."

Zoe's eyes had already picked out the name in the text as she scanned it. "Professor Ralph Henderson. Our second victim."

"Bingo," Shelley said, grabbing the papers back into a pile and shoving them into her bag. "I have his home address. Reportedly, he hasn't been able to get work for the past few months since this happened, so I imagine we will find him there."

"Then we should go," Zoe said, heading for the door herself. She did not need to turn around to know that Shelley would be right behind her.

Even if nothing else was panning out the way that she wanted it to, a solved case was a solved case. If this ex-professor was behind it all, it would be disappointing—but there would be a killer taken off the streets before any more lives were lost.

That, Zoe reminded herself as they headed for the parking garage, was what really mattered.

Even so, she couldn't shake that niggling doubt at the back of her min, that this case wasn't going to be wrapped up so easily.

Chapter Twelve

Zoe drove as Shelley worked from her laptop, hooked up to a Wi-Fi dongle. It was the most efficient way to both look up their new suspect and reach him as quickly as possible.

Zoe conceded that there was a lot to like about James Wardenford, as far as suspects went. Shelley read seven newspaper clippings to her as they drove: each told the story of a man who was used to respect, to recognition, and to a good reputation. He had lost all of it. Stronger men would have struggled to cope.

But an alcoholic?

For him, it must have sent him off the rails.

That would neatly tie a few things up. Zoe started to feel more excited about the idea, the closer they got to his home. As a theoretical physicist he would have been no stranger to complex math equations, but as a perpetual drunkard, he might have lost his ability to express them properly. Maybe he thought that what he was writing made perfect sense.

There was a little disconnect between the idea of someone so drunk they could not write correctly, yet sober enough to kill a man and leave so little evidence they had so far gotten away with it. But that was a detail Zoe was willing to let slide until they had actually spoken to him. Functioning alcoholism meant different things for different people.

They pulled up outside an apartment block, with small yet neatly maintained units clearly visible from the ground. The balconies outside each set of French doors held rose bushes in pots, bicycles, small outdoor table and chair sets. It was a nice place. The kind of building you might retire to on a modest yet comfortable pension.

The kind of place a once-well-paid professor and physicist might retreat to once his paychecks weren't so guaranteed anymore.

Apartment buildings were often a little tricky. When someone came to the front door of a house and saw the police there, they had no choice but to talk. Ringing an intercom and asking for entry meant that it could be denied.

Zoe looked up as they walked toward the front door, taking in the windows that she could see. One set of French doors was open, the curtain blowing slightly in the breeze. She made a quick calculation: third floor, fourth door along. If the building was numbered in a logical way from the left front corner, she could get them in a little easier.

She pressed three-zero-four on the intercom panel, and waited for it to connect.

Shelley was checking her notes, no doubt remembering that James Wardenford was not in fact an inhabitant of 304, but before she could protest, the call connected.

"Hello?"

"Hello, ma'am. I have a delivery."

Zoe caught Shelley's eye, shrugged, and looked back at the intercom.

"Sure, come in."

The entrance door buzzed and clicked, indicating that it had been unlocked. Zoe pushed through and started up the stairs, heading for the apartment that really did belong to their suspect.

"What are we delivering?" Shelley asked, a little primly. Rookie agents were always sticklers for the rules. Except for the ones that weren't, and ended their careers quickly. She would learn to loosen up over time.

"Justice," Zoe said, after some thought.

Shelley's peals of laughter burst through the narrow staircase, echoing from the walls. "I like that," she said, once the worst of her mirth had subsided.

The apartment was on the second floor, at the opposite side of the building from where they had come in. Zoe thought it a shame they hadn't had more opportunity to gain some clues as to Wardenford's state of mind from the exterior, but you made do with what you had. The lock on his apartment door was surrounded by scrape marks, an early clue to a habitual drunk. He missed the keyhole often, unable to see it clearly.

Zoe rapped sharply on the door as Shelley joined her, just slightly out of breath from the climb.

There was a rolling, crashing noise from within, then a few unsteady, heavy footsteps. "Jus'a minute," a male voice slurred.

"Bet he's real popular with the downstairs neighbors," Shelley muttered.

Zoe simply waited. Her patience was rewarded. James Wardenford cracked open his door without bothering to engage the safety chain, leaning on the walls of his own corridor for support as he eyed them with a squint.

He was wearing only a bathrobe one size too big for him, left open to the waist, and a pair of old, stained shorts. His feet were muffled now by worn slippers, the threadbare soles almost gone at the front. There was still a bottle of beer in his hand, two-thirds empty.

"Good morning, James Wardenford," Zoe said, deliberately raising her voice a notch. "My name is Special Agent Zoe Prime, and this is Special Agent Shelley Rose."

Normally there was a reaction at this point. The suspect would try to run somehow, or stammer, or shrink back in fear. Or they would blink far too quickly, take in rapid breaths, other signs that Zoe had come to recognize.

Wardenford, whether due to his drunken state or something else, barely reacted at all.

"Yup," he acknowledged. "Better come in while I get some clothes on."

Shelley shot Zoe a puzzled look. "We'd like to talk to you about—"

"Yeah, yeah," Wardenford said, waving a hand dismissively. "Henderson. I know. I can't go to your station, or whatever you call it, like this."

He shuffled away from the door, leaving it swinging open. Zoe hesitated for a moment, unaccustomed to such a reaction, before taking the initiative to follow him inside.

The thin foyer gave on to doors in all three directions, one of them lying open ahead. It was clearly a living area, a small sofa perched in front of a television, and Zoe ducked inside. Shelley closed the door and stayed there, nodding to Zoe when she glanced back. She would guard the exit. A wise move. It wouldn't do to have him dart past them and out to freedom while they lounged around on his sofa.

Not that his sofa was much use, Zoe saw as she approached it. There were seventeen empty beer bottles scattered on the sofa, coffee table, floor, and other odd points of the room. Among them nestled a further three whiskey bottles and four of vodka—this, then, was a man not particularly fussy about his drink so long as it did the job of getting him drunk.

There was only a foot between the edge of the coffee table and the sofa. The repeated stains on the carpet, gouges in the wood, and watermarks on the fabric of the cushions indicated that it was frequently too small a gap for an inebriated man holding a glass or bottle ready to spill or drop. Two pizza boxes were stacked haphazardly on top of the trash can, and packaging for five microwaveable meals around it. It seemed he had given up on opening the trash can to dispose of his waste after blocking access himself. Across the open-plan room, the kitchen looked pitifully underused.

The story needed no further investigation. He was an alcoholic, as they already knew, and he had clearly been binge-drinking for some time.

Wardenford emerged noisily from another of the doors in the corridor. As Zoe joined him, she gained a glimpse of a bedroom strewn with clothes and the wafting scent of old vomit.

"Right, then," he said, finishing off the last button on a crumpled shirt. "Off we go. Do you need to put handcuffs on me, or is it more informal than that?"

Zoe blinked. She had made a lot of arrests, and she had taken a lot of people in for questioning. She could not recall a single one of all those people ever volunteering to be cuffed.

"No," she said, feeling off-balance. "This is just a chat for now. But we will take you to the field office in order to record our conversation."

"Fine, fine," he said, nodding a little too aggressively. The alcohol had cut his limits, stopped telling him when to stop. "Lead on."

Over his shoulder as he walked toward the door, Zoe met Shelley's eyes. This was odd—too odd. When did a murder suspect ever just willingly, even happily, go along to the station for questioning? It was as if the man was not just resigned to his fate, but glad of it.

They walked in convoy to the car: Shelley leading, then Wardenford, then Zoe. She kept her eyes on him at all times, thinking that if he really was their guy, he was surely going to bolt. She was tense, one hand itching to rest on the holster of her gun just in case.

Nothing happened on the walk out to the parking lot. Only when he was sitting in the back of their car, with the child locks on, did Zoe allow herself a moment to relax. He wasn't going anywhere, except where they took him.

So, if he was a killer, why did he seem so pleased about that?

Zoe sat opposite James Wardenford, with Shelley in the seat next to her. The bare room—just a table and four chairs, one currently unoccupied—was dominated by one glass wall. Just like on TV, it was blacked out, impenetrable from this side. On the other side, a tech was watching closely, making sure that everything was picked up by their recording equipment.

"I knew you were coming for me," Wardenford said, scratching the back of one of his ears. He looked all the world like a man who had not a single care. They might have been chatting to him in a local grocery store about the weather, for how concerned he seemed. "It was only a matter of time, really."

"And why is that, James?" Shelley asked. She was doing her Good Cop bit. Playing the friend. It was what she was good at. Zoe, for the meantime, was content to stay quiet and observe until she had something to say.

She looked James over, reassessing as she had done so many times already. His height of five feet nine made him the correct size to have attacked the college student, Cole Davidson, at a slightly lower angle. His arms were bunched with muscles enough, though not so much to make him stand out. Still, she figured he would have had the strength for the first blow—which stunned the victims enough that they were unable to fight against the others.

It was his manner that irritated her. She knew the signs of panic or fear, the desire to not be found out. The sharp angles of the shoulders and elbows, the constant movement, the defiant lean. She had memorized all of them from textbooks before she had ever gone out into the field, and had enough experience to know now they were real.

But James Wardenford was calm and relaxed, even smiling. That did not sit well with her at all.

"The victims," Wardenford said simply. "You were always going to trace them back to me eventually."

Shelley shifted in her seat, leaning back. It seemed she was having a hard time figuring out what to make of him, too. She was switching back and forth between her usual tactics. "Is this a confession?"

James Wardenford laughed, free and easy. "Good lord, no. It just looks like me from the outside. I get that; I do. But considering I didn't do it, I'm not worried at all. Once we've cleared this all up, I'll be back at home before the day is out. It's not like I have anything better to do today."

Shelley sighed, rubbed the bridge of her nose for a moment. Zoe kept quiet. She watched him carefully, wishing she was better at reading the subtle nuances of expression and movement that gave people away.

"Let's start from the beginning, then, shall we? How does it look like you from the outside?" Shelley prompted.

"It all started with Cole Davidson, of course." Wardenford tipped his chin a few inches up, his voice increasing in volume. He was putting on a speech, as if he was addressing a lecture hall. That only unsettled Zoe further. Truthful people didn't look up that far. "Professor Henderson—Ralph—and I had, well, a bit of a falling out. You see, Cole had a bit of talent in English, or so it seemed. Ralph was absolutely determined that he ought to be kept on, to finish his studies, but he was here on a scholarship. There, I ought to say, since I don't work at the college anymore."

"What does the scholarship have to do with your falling out?"

"I'm getting to that." Wardenford's left eyebrow shot up an inch or two before dropping down. Was he actually reproaching Shelley for interrupting him? "The scholarship was dependent on Cole keeping up a certain level across all of his grades, and he was also taking my physics class. Taking being a loose word. More often than not, he slept through my lectures. Surprise surprise, he was failing."

"And Professor Henderson asked you to intervene," Shelley said. She was leaning back still, but something in her manner had changed. Zoe guessed that she had found the right tack at last. A sympathetic ear. A believer.

"More than once. We got a bit out of hand, truth be told. Ralph was in my face, telling me I couldn't possibly be doing my job correctly given the alcohol he could smell on my breath, so what did it matter if I marked the boy higher? I resented the affront to my integrity; fists were thrown. The upshot was that I was found to be drunk while teaching, and I was fired."

"How did you react to that? It must have been a blow," Shelley asked, shaking her head in solidarity.

"I went back to my old friend the bottle ever more than before. Moved out of my big house into a small apartment and made do. I haven't seen Ralph since then."

"You didn't hold a grudge against him for getting you fired?"

Wardenford studied his hands closely, taking a moment to answer. "It wasn't Ralph who got me fired. It was me. I shouldn't have been drinking at work."

There was silence for a long moment, stretching out between the three of them. Wardenford glanced up, playing into one of the oldest tricks in the book by opening his mouth to fill that silence with anything he could blurt out. "It wasn't me," he said. "Cole, nor Ralph. I had no grudge against them. I didn't even realize Cole had managed to turn things around. I thought he'd have been packed off home with his tail between his legs by now."

He wasn't going to admit to anything—that much was clear. Zoe took the moment to make her own move, finishing the formalities. "Where were you on the night Henderson was killed?"

"At home, alone—the same as the night Cole met his end. I drank until I passed out. That was probably around nine in the evening."

Zoe tilted her head slightly, a gesture of disbelief she was not quite fast enough to quash.

"I started early," Wardenford said, spreading his hands and shrugging. "I tend to. I don't have much else to fill my day, besides refreshing my inbox and wondering whether anyone is ever going to reply to any of my job applications."

"So, you have no way to prove that you were not there in the parking garage when Ralph Henderson was killed?" Zoe pressed.

Wardenford laughed again, a sound that was so out of character with their surroundings that it seemed to jar the very air. "I'm an educated man. I know as well as you do that the absence of evidence is not evidence. You have no reason to think I was anywhere near the scene, and the burden of proving that falls to you. I don't have to prove that I wasn't there if you can't prove that I was."

That rankled. More than that—it was the kind of thing you expected a career criminal to say. Someone who knew his rights because he had been in the position to have them enforced so very often. Not an innocent professor who had only recently crossed a line for the first time in his life.

"We'll take a break from this interview," Shelley said, checking her watch and starting to stand. She rattled quickly through the formalities required for the tape, before Zoe followed her out of the room and into the hidden divide behind the blacked-out glass.

Once out of sight, the two women watched their suspect, both sagging a little as they let down the pretense of not being tired and overworked.

"What do you think?" Shelley asked.

Zoe chewed on her lip for a moment before answering. "I do not trust him."

"I don't trust him either, but I do believe him."

Zoe turned, looking up to meet Shelley's eyes in surprise.

Shelley sighed. "He's a pompous ass who has seen one too many episodes of *CSI*, yes. But I think he's telling the truth. His body language, his manner—he's turning this whole thing into a joke because he feels it's below him. He sees himself as being part of a different world from ours. For him to commit a crime like that and be arrested for it would be, well, funny to him."

"Funny?" Zoe repeated, shooting a distasteful look at their suspect. "I do not think that murder is a joke."

"Poor word choice, perhaps. It's just so far from being on his radar that he could ever seriously be suspected of something like this. I really don't think he did it, Z."

Zoe hesitated, struggling to know what to believe. She didn't buy the act that Wardenford had put on—and it had been an act. That ten-degree head tilt, the orator at work. She wanted it to be him, wanted to have a solution that would put all this to bed. She wouldn't have to wrestle with those equations anymore.

But Shelley knew people, and therein lay the rub.

Who could Zoe trust—her own disbelief in his words of innocence and the lack of an alibi, or Shelley's instinct?

And what if she trusted Shelley and let him go—and he killed again?

Chapter Thirteen

He watched and moved slowly, careful not to be seen. He had left his refuge and hunkered down amongst the people at the bus stop, hiding in plain sight.

The doctor still owed him blood snakes, and he was going to get it, all right. He was going to get it, and how.

There was not much more time to wait. The doctor would be coming off shift. That was the best time to strike, oh yes. Follow him home in his refuge and strike when he was alone, get the snakes, the brains, make him pay.

The doctor came out of the building and he could barely contain his happy dance, his happy smile. He walked swiftly now, hood up against the rain, blessed rain. To his refuge and opened the door and got inside and started the engine.

He crept then, slowly on the—pathway, keeping a distance. He let the doctor go home all safe and secure, thinking he was free. Thinking he would not see his own blood snakes before the day was out. Yes, let him think that.

Let him think that, the sniveling fool, the bitter, hated enemy! How he could not wait to punish him, make him pay! How he longed for blood snakes and crushed bits of—headbox everywhere, for the doctor's last breath!

He pulled up a few doors down from the doctor's home, parking quick and ready to strike before the doctor got safe, when his—talk—walkie—buzzer rang. The display told the name of a friend.

Curses. But he had to take it.

"Hello?"

"Hey, did you hear about Wardenford?"

Alert, alarm bells, instant. The name of his mentor. Panic through his veins like an ice bolt; he knew, just *knew* something was wrong. "No?"

"He's been arrested. They're saying the FBI took him. For those murders, you know—Cole and that professor."

He could not speak. N—he could not believe it.

The friend prattled on, not realizing what he had done. "He's been on a freefall ever since Henderson got him fired. Honestly, I'm not surprised. He was always a bit of a loose cannon, wasn't he? All those outbursts?"

"It wasn't him." It came blurted out, an accident. He was desperate. How could the world think such a thing? How could the beloved professor be in the frame? No, no, no, no, no, no, no!

"You reckon? FBI wouldn't have nabbed him if they didn't think there was a good chance."

"It wasn't him."

He ended the call; couldn't stand to listen anymore. Couldn't stand the—snakes, *ear* snakes, untrue, all of them. All of them. The professor! No this, this was all wrong, all wrong.

What could he do? Let the professor be blamed? No, not that, anything but that; the professor was his favorite. He could not let the ear snakes bring down the mentor who brought him everything before this.

At least one thing was safe: he never told Wardenford about the things in his head. The accident. The cra—the cre—the crash. He never told him about the snakes in his own brain. The ones that wouldn't come out, no matter how hard he smashed. The reason why everyone else had to lose theirs.

The doctor had gone inside, out of reach. He sat and thought, in his refuge, rain drumming on the—mirror. Too late now. Doctor had to live.

Doctor living, maybe useful.

Maybe something he could do for the professor. A gift. To release him.

Clarity came for a moment, as it sometimes did. A flash of his old brilliance. A plan formed. He saw the steps that he needed to take and how he would execute them. First of all, finding a piece of evidence that should be kept protected, in a plastic bag, a thing that could be used later. Then he could continue with his original idea, make sure that the doctor paid for everything.

God, was this all a mistake? The things he had done, the way he had left them. This wasn't *him.* He didn't act like this. He wasn't a violent man. He was a scholar—none of this should ever have happened!

If it wasn't for the crash—the accident. Was it even really an accident? Everything had been destroyed at that moment, but he saw now that this was not the way to react. What had come over him? This violence, where did it come from?

But now—now Professor Wardenford was on the hook. He owed it to the professor, the person who had really believed in him, to make sure that everyone knew he was innocent. That was the right thing to do. Irrefutable proof, worse than a confession. And afterward, he could go to the police and—no—he felt it slipping. Always too soon, always destroying him again. The clarity came and then it—

He wouldn't give in. Even without the—focus, he could continue. He knew what he had to do now. It wasn't over.

Doctor dead, blood snakes released. Soon. But first the planning. First the gift to his professor. The only one who saw—future in him. The only one who thought he could be something. He would escape. But only with his help.

Doctor, doctor. Twice you slipped away.

Third time, he thought, was the—hook.

Chapter Fourteen

Zoe stood looking through the glass, studying Wardenford as closely as she could.

For the whole time he had been in custody, his demeanor had not changed. Though she found it hard to understand why, he was still casual and cheery, as if he believed that this was all a comic misunderstanding and easily cleared up. The only thing that had changed over the hours they held him was the beginning of a shake in his right hand, a telltale sign of an alcoholic in need of their next drink.

Maybe that was a weakness that she could use, at least.

"I am going back in," Zoe announced. She had grabbed up the files holding the crime scene photographs—specifically, the equations.

"Do you want me with you?" Shelley asked. She, too, had been watching for any kind of sign, while they chased surveillance footage from areas around his apartment over the phone. So far, nothing had shown him leaving his apartment. It didn't mean that he hadn't slipped by in an area not covered, but it did mean they had nothing to threaten him with.

"No." Zoe made for the door, buoyed along by a new determination. "You watch him. Closely."

"Call him professor," Shelley called after her. "You'll stroke his ego. False sense of security."

They couldn't keep him at the field office for long. A long time for him, surely, but in terms of their investigation, not long enough. If he didn't crack soon, they would have to let him leave. So, she would have to make him crack.

Zoe entered the interrogation room and resumed her seat opposite Wardenford, who greeted her with a cheery smile.

"Time to let me out yet, Agent?"

"Not yet." Zoe paused, opening the folder at such an angle that only she could see the contents. "How are you with math, Professor?"

Wardenford seemed to swell with ego as she gave him his former title. Shelley had been right. "It's one of my specialties," he said. "Of course, math goes hand in hand with physics. It's been my life's work."

Zoe nodded. "I understand," she said. "Then perhaps you can help us out with something? We have some equations that we are trying to figure out."

She first reached for the printouts she had created: the equations alone, copied out on the computer, rather than the crime scene photographs. No blood, no sign that they had anything to do with the killings. She laid them down one by one in front of him, watching his face as he leaned forward to study them.

There was no flicker of recognition in his eyes, at least not that Zoe could see. She glanced up toward the black glass wall, as if she could see through and divine what Shelley was thinking. Of course, there was nothing to see there.

Back to Wardenford; he was lifting the printouts in his hands now, comparing them side by side, rubbing his mouth and resting with his fingers over it as he leaned on his elbow. He spent longer looking at the first than the second. He frowned deeply, then deeper, the furrows on his brows lengthening and sinking.

Minutes stretched on. Zoe kept count of them: four, six, ten. He was still staring at the equations, shifting in his seat sometimes, even mouthing things to himself as he worked through them. Zoe let the silence continue, not wanting to interrupt. What he said and did now was important.

"They're unsolvable," he declared at last, throwing the two pieces of paper down onto the desk. "This is some kind of trick, isn't it?"

"Trick?" Zoe raised an eyebrow.

"You think if you can frustrate me with an equation I can't solve, I will be vulnerable to questioning and end up admitting everything. Well, I can't admit anything. I didn't do it."

"This is not a trick, Professor," Zoe said, opening her folder on the desk and spinning it toward him so that he could see it. Inside, the images were piled haphazardly: the equations scrawled out on torsos, blood, close-ups of the injuries to the heads. "We really do need to figure out those equations."

At last, there was a reaction on Wardenford's face. Not the kind of reaction that Zoe had been hoping for—a microscopic twitch, a flinch, a tiny tell that would give him away. Patterns were easy to spot in human behavior. There should have been something that told her he knew what he was looking at, and he was lying.

But there was nothing there. Just revulsion. Wardenford paled, gasped, covered his mouth. Finally, he squeezed his eyes shut and moved his head away so that he no longer had to look at them. "That's horrible," he finally managed. "Cole and—and Ralph. God. Who could do something so violent?"

"The same person who wrote out those equations." Zoe tapped the paper in front of him, drawing his attention back. "So tell me, Professor. Help us. What do they mean?"

Wardenford stole a glance at the crime scene shots and shuddered before looking down at the paper. Zoe had seen that before. People would look again and again at things they found disgusting or distressing. They couldn't help themselves.

Of course, people also looked again and again at things they were proud of.

"They don't mean anything," Wardenford said. His face was ashen now, and the cheeriness was gone entirely. In that, at least, Zoe had achieved her goal. "They ought to, but something's wrong. It's like all of the elements are there, but they've been placed incorrectly. Imbalanced. Too much on one side, not enough on the other. You won't be able to solve them or find out what they mean. They're wrong."

Zoe sighed, slumping back into her chair. It was the same as the others had said. Dr. Applewhite and her colleagues had been right, and she hadn't wanted to admit that. But it was getting harder and harder to deny that these equations weren't solvable.

At least, not yet.

"Imbalanced," she repeated, her brain starting to work.

"Yes," Wardenford confirmed. "See, here? This one should really have something *there,* but there's nothing. It doesn't make sense this way."

Imbalanced... what if that was the whole point? What if these were not individual equations to be taken separately, but part of a larger puzzle?

Zoe thought back to their last major case, to the Golden Ratio killer. His plans had seemed different at the beginning. It was only as he filled in more points on the map, took more victims, that the spiral shape became clear.

That was a terrible thought—that she might need more information. Need another death. But it did make a lot more sense than what they had already—which was nothing.

Zoe spun the two printouts toward herself and grabbed a pen from her pocket. She started to balance the equations out—adding them together. It was easy to see the spaces, now she understood to look for that kind of pattern. And it was easy to see the things on the second equation that stood out, begged to be put somewhere else.

She worked in a frenzy, forgetting that Wardenford was even in the room. This was more important than the interrogation. If he was right, this could change everything. Maybe they could work something out from this, some kind of formula, or a prediction of what the next equation would be. Any little clue along the way could help them figure out who the killer was.

That was, of course, assuming that it wasn't Wardenford and he wasn't stringing her along like a puppet, watching her dance.

Zoe paused then, looking up to see that Wardenford was watching her. Closely. She stopped writing. Perhaps that thought was right. Perhaps she was playing right into his hands, taking the bait.

"You don't see things like others do, do you?" he asked, unexpectedly.

"What?"

"I've met people like you before. You've got a way with numbers and patterns, am I right? You're a synesthete."

Zoe instinctively looked toward the darkened glass, hoping the tech had left the room. If Shelley was the only one hearing this, it wouldn't be so bad. But this was on record. Taped. Anyone could see it. She fought a rising sense of panic, her hand flying up to just below her collarbone, her neck. She felt that same stifling feeling that came when she sat in the passenger seat and the seatbelt seemed to choke her, but there was nothing there to pull away.

"I knew it. You remind me exactly of someone I mentored years ago."

Zoe was torn between anxiety over her secret being outed, and the shock that he could tell just by looking at her. "What are you talking about?" she asked, hoping it would sound like a deflection but also prompt him to explain how he had known.

"I know brilliance when I see it. You have an instinctive way of working with the numbers, and it's not just that. You're constantly assessing things, sizing them up. I can recognize it because I've seen it before."

"With your student," Zoe replied, which was not an admission, but still encouraged him to go on all the same. She was walking a dangerous line. If anyone saw this, she would have to flat-out deny it—or come clean. At least not having the admission on tape was a slim comfort.

"Yes. She was gifted—just gifted. I noticed her skills in class, and invited her for some extra sessions to see if we could coax out that genius. Lo and behold, she had capabilities I had never dreamed of. To look at a math equation and know the answer, just like that."

"What happened to her?" Zoe was desperate to know. After the news Dr. Applewhite had told her, of the student committing suicide, it was of the utmost interest to her. Had she been successful in life? Started a family, maybe?

"Ah, well, I don't really know." Wardenford coughed quietly, wearing an embarrassed expression. "I ended up quitting, you see. Coming over here to work instead. That was after my divorce; I had to get away. All my problems started there."

"That is when you began drinking."

"Right." Wardenford sighed heavily. "That's the part of the job I miss the most, you know? Nurturing young minds, helping them come to their full potential. Like you—putting the skills and talents they have to good use. Helping them to figure out what to do with the rest of their lives. I suppose all that is gone, now. No college anywhere near here is going to touch me, and I doubt I'll have a good reference if I apply elsewhere."

Maudlin self-pity. Zoe was just about to tell him to shut up and stop feeling sorry for himself, and go work on getting the things he wanted instead of drinking himself to death. Perhaps happily for her career, that was the moment that Shelley threw open the door and interrupted instead.

"Agent Rose," Zoe remarked, surprised that she would break protocol by entering the interview room. Perhaps one of their superiors had arrived, and Shelley had come to warn her…?

"Agent Prime, a word, please," Shelley said, moving back into the corridor to let Zoe out.

Once the door was firmly closed behind her and Wardenford was out of earshot, Shelley brandished her phone, indicating the source of the news that was spilling out of her. "They've found another body."

Shelley's words rolled over Zoe like a wave. There was another death. It had probably happened while Wardenford was in custody, which would mean that he was innocent.

But maybe it held another equation—another clue.

Zoe didn't know whether to be pleased or dismayed. Their phantom math killer had struck again.

But that meant there was a whole wealth of more clues waiting, any of which might help them catch him and stop him in his tracks.

Chapter Fifteen

Zoe hit the brakes, almost sending the car into a skid. She had been driving so fast down the wide, leafy suburban streets that she had almost missed the police car parked up ahead and gone right into the back of it.

They had landed outside a huge Georgian colonial, not at all out of place in this expensive neighborhood. The one thing that did set it apart were the white-suited forensics experts and uniformed police bustling outside or rushing in and out of the door in a near-perpetual routine.

Shelley was already out of her seatbelt and the door by the time Zoe had turned the engine off, and she wasn't far behind her. They both ran across the neatly kept lawn to the entrance, flashing their badges quickly at the policeman who tried to stop them approaching from the sidewalk.

The commanding officer at the scene met them at the door, knowing from a glance that they were the FBI agents he had been told to wait for.

"Agents, you're going to want to come and see this. It's a brutal one. Looks like another one of our math killer's hits."

They followed him hurriedly up a wide staircase to a master bedroom, dodging other personnel who were coming and going with fingerprint kits and DSLRs and spare evidence bags. Zoe had already counted thirteen pairs of boots on the ground. This was clearly a big deal to the locals—and of course it would be. When wealthy neighborhoods were home to violent and brutal murders, it was normally in the interest of the sheriff or chief of police to do something about it, and fast.

"Cleaner called us in when she reported for work and found the body. Thankfully she was in the habit of speaking to her employer first rather than getting right to it, so she didn't wipe any evidence away. The vic is a neurologist from the local hospital, Dr. Edwin North. Pretty well-known around these parts. He and his wife used to take part in all the community events, you know? Real pillars. His late wife, that is. Cancer last year."

This running commentary was given as they ascended the stairs, and the officer paused them outside the room itself. "I've got to tell you ladies, this is a real bad case. Maybe you shouldn't go in there. We'll have the crime scene photos along to you, but you might be better off not seeing it in person."

"We're not ladies," Shelley said, brushing by him. "We're federal agents, and I assure you we can handle it."

Zoe held back a laugh at the man's expression, and followed her. What she saw was not at all pretty. Shelley must have been fighting hard not to show any reaction, given how emotional she normally was at crime scenes.

The doctor's head was crushed, visibly so. There was an odd shape to his head, newly formed after his skull gave way under the pressure. Oblong, distorted. His eyes had bulged out under the force, his eye sockets broken at their upper edge. Brain matter and blood, along with fragments of skull, decorated the headboard.

He was lying in bed, alone, still partially covered by a blanket. He was half-dressed, giving the impression that he had stolen into the bedroom for a quick nap and nothing more. It was a nap that he was never going to wake up from again.

But most exciting of all was the link that Zoe had been waiting for. His plain shirt had been ripped open, traces of blood still clinging to it where it had been thrown aside. Across his bare torso, another equation was written in thick black numbers and letters.

The blood was still wet. He had been killed in the last hour or less. Even as they watched, a small piece of brain matter that had attached itself to the wall slowly peeled away and dropped down. This crime scene was still settling into place.

This had happened while they were at James Wardenford's home, arresting him, or at least in the minutes before or after. No way he could have got home, washed himself off, and played the part of the drunkard in time. Even the first part would have been too much of a stretch, given the distance between the homes. Wardenford was in the clear.

Shelley was taking it all in, breathing through her mouth rather than her nose, and Zoe took that as her cue. She was long used to gruesome scenes like these, and it was all just meat to her. Better that she take the lead while Shelley found her feet.

"What was his schedule for today?" Zoe asked.

The policeman flipped back a page in his notebook. "He finished his last shift early this morning, and then was due back in this evening at nine to handle a late shift. Looks like he was getting some shut-eye beforehand."

Shelley had recovered enough to draw closer to the body. "Any initial forensics reports?"

The officer followed her, leaning in to point at various parts of the skull with an outstretched pen. "They tell me the doctor was stunned first with a single blow, here. We can only just see the edge of the impact mark under all the rest of it, but it was likely solidly across the front of his head. Enough that even if he woke up, he'd have been out of it. Difficult for him to fight back at all."

Shelley nodded, while Zoe ranged around the room, careful where she stepped. She was making calculations. She knew it took around a thousand pounds of force to cause the average skull fracture. Their killer certainly was not heavy or strong enough to provide that force himself—so he must have used something heavy, and thrown it down on top of the victim's head.

"Have you recovered the weapon?" she asked.

Their guide, as well as the three forensics officials still working in the room, all shook their heads.

"Heavy, but thin," Shelley suggested, studying the impact marks on the man's face.

Zoe nodded approvingly. "No wider than my hand. Dropped three or four times, with decreasing force each time. Our killer was running out of strength."

"Then, did he bring it with him? Or take it from the house?"

Zoe thought that over. "Interesting question. Either he planned in advance very carefully, or he took an opportunity when he found one. What do we think?"

"He seems like both. It's a paradox, this case. Planned and premeditated—he waited for the professor. Took the student somewhere that wasn't covered by surveillance. But the killings themselves are rage-driven, spontaneous. Using the environment."

"How did he get in?" Zoe directed her question at the officer.

"Back door had been sabotaged. It's almost as old as the house, beautiful wood paneling. Someone carefully and slowly sawed through it, put their hand through one of the panels, and turned the key from the outside to let themselves in. The doctor had ambient noise playing in here over his smart speakers. He wouldn't have heard a thing, I don't think."

Zoe was done with the scene; she knew everything she needed to, from there at least. Nothing contradicted her earlier thoughts that the killer would be five foot nine, of average build, but perhaps a little muscular. Now she could let herself indulge in the one thing she was really interested in.

She took out her phone and started taking photographs of the equation, angling herself in to get the best shots. Shelley and the others in the room continued low conversations, but Zoe tuned them out, only keeping herself vaguely aware of what they were saying in case something important came up.

The shots taken, Zoe drifted down out of the room and down the corridor, lightly nudging the next door open with her elbow so as to avoid touching the handle. There was light afternoon sun streaming through the large windows, illuminating a miniature gym room with a treadmill set up to face the view.

Zoe moved past it, examining the other items. A large blue balance ball, several straps and lengths of stretchy material used for strength training. A rowing machine, low on the ground, with an empty water bottle still fitted into the appropriate slot.

Weights, stacked up against the far wall. Zoe counted their number and value, noted the thicker layer of dust on the bottom weights—the heaviest—compared to the top. By the pyramid-like stand was a bar, the kind you thought of when you imagined old-fashioned weightlifters. There were several flat, circular weights stacked beside it, evidently used to increase or decrease the weight on the bar as you wished.

Zoe crouched, her attention suddenly caught by something. And yes—there it was. On the edge of one of the larger weights, concentrated much more in one area with almost nothing further along the circle. Blood and fragments of brain and skull.

"In here!" she shouted, sure now that she was looking at the murder weapon.

Shelley arrived fast, the forensics people hot on her heels. Zoe moved out of the way to allow them in, pointing out the incriminating evidence. She looked over the rest of the room more closely, seeking another sign of their killer's presence. A footprint in undisturbed dust, a smudge from a finger, anything that would help.

"What are these here?"

Shelley's voice snapped Zoe out of her concentration. The forensics team rushed over to where Shelley was pointing, on the floor just by the dropped weight.

"Strands of hair," one of them muttered, taking out an evidence bag. "Very short. Well spotted."

"It could be the victim's," another of them pointed out, his voice muffled by the mask he wore over his mouth.

"One dark and one gray," Shelley said. "The victim looks to have been blond. From here, at least."

The two hairs were lifted with fine tweezers, dropped into the waiting evidence bag, and marked. "We'll have them analyzed. With any luck, there will be enough of the hair follicle on there to get us a match."

"We might have our killer," Shelley said, with such obvious glee that it sent a thrill up Zoe's spine. She was right. That kind of break could crack the whole case wide open, give them a name. Once they had that, they could get him in for questioning, get him to tell them everything. Hairs weren't always worth what they used to be in a courtroom, but a confession was.

And this was exactly the kind of evidence that Zoe knew Shelley could put to good use in extracting a confession.

All the tools they needed to close the case may already have been sitting in that evidence bag.

Chapter Sixteen

Zoe walked back into the interrogation room, holding a fresh set of color prints that were still warm from the machine that had spit them out.

"Oh, you're back," Wardenford said. "I thought you might have forgotten about me."

Zoe eyed his hands and spotted the telltale shake. He was no doubt anxious to get out of FBI custody and go home for a drink. He'd been with them for hours now, and he was a serious alcoholic. The ratio in his bloodstream was decreasing, leaving behind the physical symptoms he would no doubt do anything to avoid.

Zoe had done anything but forget about Wardenford. During the drive back to HQ, she had formulated a plan. Shelley would go to the forensics lab and encourage a rush on the hair that they had found, using her natural charm to get it done quicker than Zoe could. Meanwhile, Zoe would talk to their former suspect.

Maybe it was obvious now that he was innocent of being the killer, but that didn't mean they needed to let him go right away. He had been able to glean something, at least, from the equations—and he had spotted Zoe's abilities right away. That meant that, for now at least, he was an asset.

An asset who could help them with this latest piece of the puzzle.

"Take a look at these," Zoe said, dropping the photographs in front of him and taking her seat.

She was banking on the fact that Wardenford would be distracted enough by the allure of the mathematical puzzle to not notice that he had now been proven innocent. Just as she herself would not be able to resist attempting to work it out. True to form, he snatched up the pictures immediately, his lips moving silently as his eyes traced over the new equation.

Zoe watched him carefully as she had before. There was still no flicker of recognition, not that she could see; only eagerness to take on a challenge. She had harbored the small suspicion that Wardenford could still have been involved, with an accomplice taking down North, but now that was gone. His reaction coupled with the shaking of his hands, which were not steady enough to tackle a victim or write out a clear equation, told her everything that she needed to know.

Dr. Edwin North's family and colleagues may hold more answers. Shelley would move on to talking with them after she had visited the lab, but Zoe wanted to be here. Working on this. She still felt that this was the most important part of it all—that putting the equations together might reveal a larger solution, something that required lengthy workings and complex enough math to stump even the experts.

Even Zoe, until, she hoped, enough was revealed to facilitate that breakthrough.

The only sound in the interrogation room was the ticking of the clock above the door and a slight shuffle of papers now and then, as Zoe and Wardenford both studied copies of the photographs in silence. The equation was just as before: seeming to make sense up to a point, then disintegrating into nonsense. There was a mismatch somewhere, something that did not fit.

"It's wrong," Wardenford eventually declared, planting his hands firmly onto the tabletop to hide their shaking. "Just the same as the other two. The last part is broken."

Zoe had already reached the same conclusion, but there was something about what he said that drew her attention. "The last part?"

"Yes, the final three lines. Look at them—they're totally unbalanced against the rest of it. This one even switches to different symbols. Where is N in those lines? The first section seems weighted towards using N as a crucial part of the equations, where it does not appear at all in the end part."

Zoe cast her eyes over the equation again, though her memory had already told her he was right. The last three lines... was there something in that?

Seized by a sudden inspiration, she flipped back through her notebook to where she had written out the first two equations. "There must be a connection between all three," she said.

"That's a false equivalency," Wardenford shook his head. "Just because the same person wrote the three equations on bodies in the same way, does not necessarily mean that they are part of the same overarching equation or connected in a further way."

Zoe could not listen to him. How could she? If he was right, then there was no way to solve the equations. And if there was no way to solve them, then there was no extra clue hiding in there which would help her to link the three victims and trace the link back to the killer.

There had to be some kind of connection.

There just had to be.

"You're wasting your time," Wardenford insisted, but Zoe was no longer hearing him. She started to scribble out the last three lines of each of the equations on the back of one of the photographs, in order. Just the last three lines, the three that didn't make any sense in each of the cases.

When she was done, she stopped and looked at it. It made a full equation in itself, and now the signs were starting to make sense. This was something that she could understand, at last. This was something—somehow—familiar?

Wardenford reached for the paper and spun it around so that he could read it, his eyes flashing from left to right over and over. It was beginning to dawn on Zoe exactly why that equation looked familiar, something rushing through the synapses in her brain to tell her just where she had seen it before—

And, oh. Oh no.

"I've seen this before," Wardenford said, even as Zoe's mouth opened to cut him off, to tell him to stop. "It's a theoretical equation that a local mathematician came up with. It made quite a stir, actually. Her name was something—what was it now? Apple . . . Applewhite. Dr. Applewhite, that was it. This is her equation, in full."

Zoe knew now what she had done. It was clear. She had been desperate for a way to make sense of it all, and so she had fallen back on something that she recognized. Just like how other people supposedly saw a face on the moon, instead of measurable craters and hills and valleys. There was no face on the moon.

In just the same sense, there was no way that Dr. Applewhite really had anything to do with this.

It couldn't be right—it was all just a coincidence. Maybe Zoe had even copied out the equations incorrectly. She flipped back in her notebook, checking and rechecking.

"That's your culprit, then," Wardenford pronounced, leaning back in his chair and folding his arms at ninety-degree angles across a puffed-up chest. "Dr. Applewhite. She's got offices somewhere nearby, does studies on people with abilities like yours. Hang on, you probably know her, don't you? She must have finally cracked."

Zoe's mind was racing, trying to find a possibility which explained all of this. Coincidences happened, even if they were not statistically likely. In fact, that's all they were: the collision of things that were somewhat likely, happening in an order which was less likely and yet still possible. In an infinite universe, everything that was possible to happen *would* happen. That was the theory, wasn't it?

"This cannot be anything to do with Dr. Applewhite," Zoe blurted out abruptly, pushing all of the photographs together into a messy pile that she could scoop up into her arms. "You are no longer a suspect, Mr. Wardenford. You are free to go. See them at the front desk about getting a taxi."

She rushed out of the room, opening the door awkwardly with one hand holding the bundle of images against her chest, and almost collided with Shelley in the corridor.

"In here," Shelley said, her voice harder and flatter than Zoe had ever heard it before. She barely had time to register what was going on before they were both sealed away in the observation room adjoining the interrogation room, where on the other side of the black glass James Wardenford was getting up to leave.

"How much of that did you hear?" Zoe asked, hating the tremor in her voice as she asked it. Hating the fact that there was something she hadn't wanted anyone to hear at all.

"More than enough," Shelley said, shaking her head. "Zoe, there's something else you need to know. Forensics already came back on those hair follicles. They didn't get a match in our database."

"That does not mean anything," Zoe pointed out. "Only that our suspect has not been previously arrested. We will be able to find a suspect eventually, and then we can test them against the hairs."

"We already have a suspect," Shelley said. Her voice was low and soft, but Zoe still flinched away when Shelley reached out to put a hand on her upper arm. "Z, we have to follow through on this lead. You know we do. We have a professional obligation."

"There is no lead," Zoe snapped. "I simply wrote it down wrong. I will go back to our files and work out where I went wrong. There is absolutely no real connection here. Taking a sample slice out of the equations—you could make them resemble anything, if you wanted to."

"I know you don't want to see it," Shelley said. Her tone was still soothing, but there was a determination in her eyes that Zoe understood fully. There was no getting away from this. "Call Dr. Applewhite and find out where she is. We have a responsibility to ask her to submit to a DNA test."

"It will not show anything. She is not connected, not in any way," Zoe argued hopelessly. She knew that Shelley was right. She wouldn't even be able to submit paperwork omitting this without risking her job. She could even go to court for withholding something this serious.

"Then she will be ruled out. But, Z, you should prepare yourself." Shelley gave her a stern look. "We have to obtain a DNA sample from Dr. Applewhite. And if it matches, we will have to arrest her for murder."

Chapter Seventeen

Zoe had a sick ache in the pit of her stomach. She couldn't tell whether she was about to throw up, lie down and die, or give birth to some kind of monstrous child. The feeling had been growing by the second since Shelley had laid down the law, and now it was threatening to totally consume her.

Zoe had had no intention of implicating anyone, especially not her beloved mentor. She could see clearly that it had all been her own mistake. There was no connection—truly, none at all.

She just couldn't get Shelley to see that.

Ultimately, it didn't matter what either of them believed. The wheels were in motion now, and procedure dictated that they follow every possible lead. If they were found not to have followed this through later, they could both lose their jobs—and it could even jeopardize the case once they brought the real killer to trial. Defense lawyers loved nothing more than loose ends.

Zoe didn't need to call Dr. Applewhite to know where she would be: in her office, as she was every day at this time. Likely meeting with someone from her case study group. She was a busy woman, and this interruption to her working hours would no doubt cause her no end of hassle. Zoe felt guilty even to be bringing this to her door. With every minute that passed, she was thinking up another reason why this was quite possibly the worst thing that she had ever done.

"How can I help you?" the bespectacled receptionist in the cool white room that served as Dr. Applewhite's foyer asked them, if not with suspicion, then certainly with curiosity. She must have known that no one was due to come in at that moment.

"We need to speak with Dr. Applewhite," Zoe said, feeling bile rise in her throat as she said the words.

"She's occupied at the moment," the receptionist said, glancing up to check the clock. "She'll be out in about twenty-five minutes, I should think."

Shelley took out her badge and laid it on the desk for a moment, keeping her fingertips in contact. "It's rather urgent," she said.

The receptionist's mouth formed a shocked "oh" of nude lipstick, and she was reaching for an internal phone when Zoe stopped her.

"We will wait," she said, gesturing to the nearby chairs for Shelley's benefit. The last thing that she wanted to do was to embarrass Dr. Applewhite by bursting in on something scheduled. Especially given that this was nothing at all to do with her, and only Zoe's own mistake. Dr. Applewhite could not be anything but innocent. There was not even the shadow of a doubt in Zoe's mind that this was all about to be cleared up, albeit painfully and awkwardly. It was that part that she was dreading.

The minutes ticked by interminably. Even for Zoe, who normally had an impeccable inner clock, it seemed to drag on for hours. Then there were only ten minutes to go, and she began to really sweat about what was to come. As soon as that happened, time altered itself again: ten minutes flashed by so fast that Zoe had to double-check her watch when Dr. Applewhite's door opened.

"Great work. I'll see you next week," Dr. Applewhite was saying, ushering a young man out into the waiting room. He ambled past them with a curious look, even glancing back over his shoulder as he heard Dr. Applewhite greeting her former charge.

"Zoe! What brings you here? More news on the case already?"

Zoe could barely look her in the eye as she got up from her seat, nodding her head. "There has been an update. We have a new body, with a new equation."

"Do you have a copy for me to look at?" Dr. Applewhite asked. Her head was swinging from Zoe to Shelley, no doubt confused by their unhappy expressions. It was like a pendulum in a clock, ticking onward almost at an even rate of seconds. Tick. Tick. Tick.

"It would be better if we could talk to you in a more private setting," Shelley said tactfully.

"We can use my office." Dr. Applewhite gestured back toward the open door, and even took a few steps back before Shelley interrupted her.

"No. We'd be better off in our office, so to speak. We need to ask you to provide a voluntary DNA sample."

Dr. Applewhite paused, looking over at Zoe. Zoe looked up and met her eyes, and instantly wished that she hadn't.

"What is this about?" Dr. Applewhite asked, her tone less sure now.

"We need to eliminate you from the case," Shelley said, simply.

Dr. Applewhite was still looking to Zoe, as if waiting for confirmation. All she could do was give a single, sharp nod, the shame weighing heavy on the back of her neck.

"All right," Dr. Applewhite conceded, uncertainty flooding her voice. She glanced over to her open-mouthed receptionist and nodded to her, receiving a nod in return as the other woman began shuffling through an appointment book.

Zoe allowed Dr. Applewhite to walk out of the office first, Shelley behind, with Zoe trailing last. This was the last thing that she wanted. She just hoped that it would be over quickly, so that she could apologize and make it right.

⚜ ⚜ ⚜

Zoe watched uncomfortably as Dr. Applewhite held her mouth open for a swab, through the glass window of a door in the lab area of the J. Edgar Hoover Building.

"I do not like this," she muttered, just loud enough for Shelley to hear her.

"I know you don't," Shelley said, holding back what Zoe imagined was the internal *you've made that pretty clear.* "Let's just hope that it clears her and we can move on to some other angle."

Zoe gritted her teeth, keeping her mouth shut. Shelley was right. That was all they could do, now; wait for the results and hope.

"All done." The lab tech, a woman in her mid-fifties called Anjali, poked her head through the door.

"Great. How long will it take?" Shelley asked.

Anjali twisted her mouth. "I've already fast-tracked one sample for you today, Shelley. We do have other cases on the roster, you know."

"I know, but this is a local case," Shelley said. "Your boy goes to the college, doesn't he? Jaipinder? All the attacks so far have been on campus. The quicker we get this case wrapped up, the better."

Anjali rolled her eyes at the obvious emotional blackmail, but nodded all the same. "I will get it through as quick as I can. No promises, though."

"Thank you, Anjali." Shelley smiled, offering her colleague a one-second shoulder squeeze as Dr. Applewhite joined them in the corridor.

With Anjali retreating back toward her office, Zoe turned to her mentor and gave her a nod of solidarity. "That is all we need for now. You can go home."

"Wh—no, it isn't," Shelley interrupted, seemingly lost for words for a moment. "We still have a lot of questions. About the equations, for example. And we can't just let a suspect go home without due diligence."

Dr. Applewhite's eyebrows shot up an inch at the use of the word "suspect."

"That will not be necessary," Zoe said, turning to face Shelley head-on. "I am vouching for her. She will not flee the country or go on a murder spree. We can call and let her know when the results have cleared her."

"Zoe," Shelley said, then caught herself and lowered her tone. She pulled Zoe's sleeve to angle them both away from Applewhite, facing down the corridor where they could discuss more discreetly. "That's against protocol. I know you have history, but that doesn't matter. We do this by the book. If you get caught giving preferential treatment, we'll be off the case at the very least."

"She did not do anything wrong," Zoe insisted. There was a stubborn streak in her a mile long, and Shelley had yet to come up against that. She was in for a surprise if she wanted to test it.

It was Zoe and Dr. Applewhite against the world now, and she wasn't going to let her down. Not when Dr. Applewhite had been the only person who always had her back. She was going to fight on her behalf, and she couldn't stand hearing the accusation and the suspicion.

"Even if she didn't," Shelley said, pausing with an emphasis that seemed to suggest that she was not convinced, "we still need to keep her here. Tick the boxes. This is the way we work cases, Z, and you know that. We don't get to break the procedure just because we know someone personally."

Zoe opened her mouth to reply, but she never had a chance.

"If I may interrupt," Dr. Applewhite said, her tone mild. "I don't mind staying until this is sorted out. Really, it's no problem. I've already cancelled my appointments for the rest of the day, so I have nothing to rush back to."

"But," Zoe began, about to protest on her behalf.

"It's really fine," Dr. Applewhite said, firmly and with a meaningful glance her way. "I mean it. I have nothing to hide, so what's the harm?"

Zoe's shoulders slumped, and she couldn't quite bear to face Shelley as she nodded assent.

The three of them marched silently back through the corridors of the J. Edgar Hoover building, out of the labs and back toward the holding rooms, to a place where they could leave Dr. Applewhite for a few hours. They took the turns and chose the right floor in the lift without discussion. Zoe did not feel up to interrogating Dr. Applewhite about the equations, and she couldn't imagine that Shelley wanted to at that moment either.

Instead she counted their steps, listening to the rhythm and cadence of a pair of heels and two pairs of flats. The harder, heavier thud of her own boots, the slightly faster patter of Shelley's dress shoes, her stride shorter than that of the other two women. The pattern that echoed against the walls as they fell more or less into step with one another, as humans who walk together are wont to do.

Zoe stayed out in the hall when Shelley showed Dr. Applewhite into the questioning room where she would wait for them, and asked her about wanting a drink, and made sure that she was seated comfortably. She stared straight ahead down toward the next bend, and hated herself for flinching when Shelley closed the door and locked it.

"I know you aren't happy with me right now," Shelley sighed. "But it's only for a few hours. Like you said, she's innocent. Once we have this done, we can move on to other things. Maybe someone's targeting Dr. Applewhite by pointing to her equations. Who knows? Maybe they were there as a clue, and we just saved her life by keeping her in a secure building while the killer waits outside her apartment."

That was some consolation, but it did put a shiver down Zoe's spine. "You think we should assign her a police escort when she leaves? Make sure that no one is stalking her?"

"It's worth thinking about." Shelley cocked her head and smiled at Zoe in a way she didn't totally understand. "You know, there's one nice thing come out of all this. I feel like I'm getting to know you better. I didn't know you had someone you felt so strongly about."

Zoe was taken aback by the observation. She looked toward the door, even as she knew that there was no way Dr. Applewhite could hear them through the reinforced material. "I... I suppose we are close. Dr. Applewhite was the first person to... diagnose me. She supported me."

"I know it can't be easy seeing her in here." Shelley sighed and gestured to the next door along the hall. "Come on. We can sit on the observation side and wait for the call. Keep her company, of a sorts."

After several hours of continued staring at the equations, Zoe was still no closer to figuring it all out than she had been the first moment they were handed the case. No matter how she looked at them, she couldn't figure out how they worked or even why they were broken. And worse: the more she looked, the less convinced she was that it really was a coincidence. Those last lines made a perfect copy of Dr. Applewhite's theory.

That kind of thing didn't happen by accident.

Shelley's cell rang, and the two of them snapped to attention. They looked at it for a second, buzzing on the ledge in front of them, before Shelley grabbed it and answered.

"Hello, Anjali? Yes... Right. And you're absolutely sure? Okay, thank you. Yes, I do owe you one. Well, all right, two. Thanks again."

Shelley finished the call and put her cell down, biting her lip. She hadn't taken her eyes off it yet, or looked up any higher than Zoe's knee since she had answered it.

Zoe, who had observed that Shelley spent around seventy-five percent of her time looking at people's faces, and perhaps thirty percent looking someone directly in the eye, considered this to be a very bad sign indeed.

Shelley's face was pale when she did look up, and then she had to glance away again before she spoke. "The DNA is a match."

Zoe waited for a moment for the punchline or an explanation. When Shelley didn't say anything else, she had to follow up with a prompt. "A match for what?"

"For Dr. Applewhite. The hairs are hers."

There was no response in Zoe's head. Only silence. She sat there looking at Shelley, the words ringing hollow in the room around them, nothing but utter disbelief bouncing back.

Chapter Eighteen

Zoe could barely gather her wits to figure any of this out. What did it all mean? Not for a single second did she believe it, no matter what the evidence said. There had to be some kind of mistake—some kind of trick.

"I'll go tell her the news, and give her a formal charge." Shelley was already standing, making the move to go forward.

In movies and on TV, this was the moment where the protagonist bravely stepped forward. "No," they would say, putting on a serious face. "I'll do it." Then they would stride forward and deliver the bad news to their loved one, or the bullet, depending on what kind of show it was.

But Zoe wasn't particularly brave, and she knew she couldn't bear to tell Dr. Applewhite that she was now under firm suspicion for the murders of three people. Worse, she couldn't even trust herself not to leave the door open and encourage her mentor to make an exit. Even if Dr. Applewhite was too honorable to do such a thing, Zoe would make the offer. That was enough to get her into deep trouble.

So, she watched as Shelley entered the room on the other side of the black glass, and as Dr. Applewhite looked up in hope of being released. She heard Shelley deliver the news, and she watched the effect on her friend in real time: the confusion, the shock, and finally, the realization that she was not going home any time soon.

As if she knew that Zoe was watching, Dr. Applewhite turned to the one-way mirror and looked at what must have been her own reflection, her mouth opening and closing silently with questions of doubt and protests, and Zoe felt even more shame that she hadn't been able to find it in herself to go in there.

"This is Ralph Henderson," Shelley said, sliding a printed color photograph across the table to Dr. Applewhite. "Do you recognize him?"

"Well, yes," Dr. Applewhite said, finally wrenching her attention away from the glass. "We're colleagues. I've seen him at faculty events, and around campus. And—well—in the news, recently."

Shelley slid another photograph towards her. "How about this man?"

"Cole Davidson." Dr. Applewhite swallowed hard. "A grad student. I tutored him for a while."

"And this one?"

"I co-authored a study with Dr. North last year," Dr. Applewhite said, her face visibly pale. "Wait, Edwin is—is he dead? I—I hadn't heard…"

"Dr. Francesca Applewhite, you are now under arrest for suspicion of murder." Shelley was reciting the lines from long-learned rote, but Zoe saw that her hands were clenched into tight fists at her sides. "You have the right to remain silent. Anything you say can be used against you in court. You have the right to talk to a lawyer for advice before we ask you any questions. You have the right to have a lawyer with you during questioning. If you cannot afford a lawyer, one will be appointed for you before any questioning if you wish. If you decide to answer questions now without a lawyer present, you have the right to stop answering at any time. Do you understand?"

"Yes," Dr. Applewhite breathed, seemingly incapable of more.

"Do you wish to call a lawyer, or have us call one for you?"

Zoe barely heard what they were saying. Her mind was racing, so fast that everything else around her was disappearing. She paid no attention to what her eyes saw or her ears heard, or her body felt. She was thinking about the case.

Thinking about how it could be that an innocent woman's hair ended up at a crime scene, right next to a dead body.

It had to be wrong somehow, didn't it? It had to be a red herring. There was no way that Dr. Applewhite had done anything. Zoe's opinion on that had not changed. No matter what, she wouldn't allow herself to doubt her.

And again, it circled around in her mind that this was all her fault. If she hadn't taken the equation apart and put it back together—right in front of a local mathematician, one of few people who would actually recognize the shape she had made—then Dr. Applewhite would never even have been a person of interest. They wouldn't have needed to take her DNA.

Maybe Zoe should have stood up to Shelley a little more, too. Made it clear to her that there was no way they were going to even slightly suspect

Dr. Applewhite, insist on putting off the DNA swabs. Surely, she should have done *something*.

"You got a handle on this, Z?"

Zoe looked up to realize that Shelley was back in the observation area with her. On the other side of the glass, Dr. Applewhite was sitting alone in a locked room.

"It is not her," she said, immediately.

Shelley sighed, her fingers searching for and twisting the small silver arrow she wore on a chain around her neck. "I know you're sure, Z, but I don't know her," she said. "I have to go with the evidence. How would her hairs get into that room, if she's not the killer?"

"I do not know, yet. But she has no motive. You have to see that."

"No motive, but we have connections to each one of the victims. That means a motive might be lurking just beneath the surface. Don't... don't get mad at me, Zoe. I'm just trying to look at this objectively. In any other case, we'd be sure we had our perp."

"No, we would not." Zoe was hit by a sudden realization, a lightbulb moment of inspiration that was as dazzling as it was relief-granting. "I would have dismissed her as a suspect immediately. The numbers do not add up."

"The equation?" A deep crease appeared across three inches of Shelley's forehead. "But I thought—"

"Not the equation. The crime scenes." Zoe stood, feeling adrenaline rush through her. She had figured it out. "My calculations at each of the scenes indicate a killer with a height of five foot nine. Dr. Applewhite is only five foot six. What is more, she weighs one hundred and twenty-nine pounds, while the killer must be over one hundred and thirty-five. There is also the consideration of the weights at Dr. North's home. I do not believe that Dr. Applewhite would be able to lift them."

As each fact hit home, Shelley's expression became less and less sure, until she finally sank down into a chair next to Zoe. "All right, I believe you," she said. "But there's still a problem. We can't just let her go."

"Why not? I have just proven that she is not—"

"Yes, I know. And I *do* believe you. But how are we going to explain that to anyone else? You won't let me tell anyone about your numbers thing, and that's even before the issue of convincing people that it works every time. There's evidence here. Cops don't just ignore evidence. FBI agents can't just let people go without questioning on a hunch. Even if I was fully behind letting her out—Z, we can't. We'd have to explain it to SAIC Maitland. Probably in a court of law one day, too."

Zoe thought this over, another idea forming in her head already. "All right," she agreed, nodding slowly. "So, then we will question her."

She smiled, and though Shelley met her with a baffled look, Zoe was starting to feel more confident by the second.

Zoe took a steadying breath and tried to ignore their surroundings. She still felt awful that Dr. Applewhite was having to sit in this bare, uncomfortable room for any longer than she already had. She still had not forgiven herself for putting her mentor there in the first place. But at least this way, she could try to make it all worthwhile.

"So, Dr. Applewhite," she began, her eyes seeking out the red light that indicated the recorder was rolling, "you have indicated to us that you are happy to answer a few questions without a lawyer present."

"I don't need legal representation. I haven't done anything wrong." Dr. Applewhite, too, seemed to have gained some strength from knowing that Zoe would be the one to question her. She had raised her chin a couple of inches higher, and the valleys and hills around her forehead and eyes had cleared. There was only the faintest hint of a tremble in her hands as she raised one to touch her hair.

That, too, was something that Zoe had decided she was not going to forgive herself for.

"We should talk about your whereabouts during the past week. I have some specific dates and times."

"I keep a set schedule," Dr. Applewhite replied. "Home in the evenings, after a day of classes or patients or research groups. My receptionist has a record of everything."

"Your husband was at home?"

A shadow passed over Dr. Applewhite's face, her eyes searching for something on the tabletop for a brief second. "He's often home late. Sometimes he stays at an apartment on the other side of the city. When he's working so late there's no sense in driving back."

Silence rested between them for a moment. It wasn't good. If Dr. Applewhite had had a strong alibi, Zoe could have released her almost immediately. That wasn't going to happen.

"I didn't do it," Dr. Applewhite said suddenly, leaning forward over the table at an acute angle. "Any of it. I'm not that kind of person, Zoe. I'm not a killer. I couldn't." There was emotion in her voice, but she seemed calm. Clear and direct.

"I know," Zoe said, her eyes flicking unbidden to that red light. She shouldn't have said that. It could be brought up in court—the prosecution might allege that other suspects weren't treated seriously, once they did bring the real killer to justice. Zoe sat up a little straighter, thinking that a change of subject might help. "Tell me about the equation."

Dr. Applewhite nodded, taking the changed tack with focus. "It's a theoretical equation I came up with a little while ago. I spend a lot of time working with colleagues in mathematics circles, not to mention certain—gifted individuals." Her eyes conveyed what her tone did not; that Zoe was one such. "It helps me keep in shape, so to speak, to work on these kinds of projects in my spare time. Anyway, I published it, and I suppose it generated a bit of buzz in local circles. It wouldn't be much known outside of this area, but at the college, we discussed it in depth."

That caught Zoe's attention. It narrowed their suspect pool significantly. The killer had to be a local. Not only to get access to the victims and know who they were, but to recognize the equation—if, indeed, it had not appeared by coincidence.

But the hairs, too—it was beginning to look more and more like an attempt to frame Dr. Applewhite. Which meant it had to be someone who knew her, and knew her now—not some random from her past who would never have heard of the equation.

"Do you have any enemies, Dr. Applewhite? Anyone who might hold a grudge against you?"

Dr. Applewhite blinked at the change in her line of questioning. "I don't believe so. I don't particularly do any kind of controversial work. I had a research subject pass away recently, unfortunately, after taking his own life. I haven't felt any indication of blame from their family, however."

"And in the world of math?"

Dr. Applewhite shook her head slowly, side to side, three times. "No. I've never…done anything. The equation was a bit of fun, really, nothing more. I wasn't going after someone else's project or stepping on any toes. Besides, it wasn't exactly a success. I could never quite get it finished off."

That sparked Zoe's attention. "Your equation is not complete?"

"That's why I published it in the first place." Despite the circumstances, Dr. Applewhite managed a small and thin-lipped smile as she tucked a strand of bobbed dark hair behind her ears. "I am not a genius at these things. I have studied, but I am not as gifted as others. I thought that if I shared it, someone else might be able to make the necessary corrections and get it finished off."

All of this was extremely interesting, and more so by the minute. Zoe looked off to the side of the room thoughtfully, turning it over in her mind. Dr. Applewhite writes an equation that she knows is flawed; it turns up on the dead bodies of men all connected to her, with evidence seemingly linked to the scene. More than that, it shows up in equations which are themselves seemingly flawed.

What did it all mean?

Zoe looked into her mentor's eyes and threw caution to the wind. Tape be damned. She wasn't going to let Dr. Applewhite sit here, afraid for her future and her freedom, without a word of reassurance. "I am going to do everything that I can to get you out of here," she said, firmly and without hesitation. "You can bet on that. I will find the real killer."

Zoe got up and headed for the door. The interview was over. She had work to do—and she was going to clear Dr. Applewhite's name sooner rather than later. She wasn't about to sit around wasting time.

Chapter Nineteen

Shelley watched their exchange with bated breath, twisting her pendant around in her fingers and anxiously listening as Zoe said things she shouldn't have been saying on tape. It was only when she tasted cold metal in her mouth that she realized she had retreated to a habit she thought she had kicked back in high school—chewing her fingernails.

Shelley pulled her hand away from her mouth, and tutted at herself to see smears of pink lipstick on her skin. She would ask herself what she had been thinking, but the answer was clearly not very much.

Grabbing a tissue out of her pocket to wipe the marks away, Shelley caught sight of the time as her smartwatch lit up. It was getting late. Far too late, now, to really get things cleared up and dealt with before they had to stop for the night.

It looked like Dr. Applewhite wasn't going to be going home to her own bed.

Shelley was just thinking about going in and interrupting when Zoe finished the interview, in that abrupt way of hers, and strode out of the room. Despite the show of confidence, Shelley wasn't sure that Zoe was dealing with all of this well. It was hard to tell, given that Zoe almost always wore the same mask of dispassionate concentration, but Shelley knew how to read people. She was even, after spending more and more time working with her, starting to be able to read Zoe.

"Where are you going in a hurry?" Shelley asked, as Zoe burst into the observation room, grabbed her coat, and turned on her heel.

"There is more investigation to be done." Zoe was already halfway out into the corridor. "I am going to reexamine all of the evidence."

"All of it?" Shelley shot to her feet and followed after her, managing to grab her arm and hold her still for a moment.

"Yes. Why would I not be thorough?"

By the way Zoe was looking at her, Shelley had a feeling that she hadn't looked at a clock in a while. "Zoe, it's late. We need to leave this for the night and get Dr. Applewhite to a holding cell. In the morning, we can start fresh."

"We cannot leave!" Zoe gaped, seemingly horrified. "She is stuck in there until we clear her name."

"I know, Z. But we aren't going to get her cleared tonight. Besides, there's proper procedure to follow. You can't just leave her in for questioning all night long and pop in and out whenever something occurs to you."

Zoe was deflating, her sense of purpose beginning to drain away. This was what Shelley had been afraid of. Though someone else might not have seen it, she could. Guilt was eating away at Zoe—and fear. Fear that she wouldn't be able to do anything to get Dr. Applewhite cleared. For someone like Zoe, those heavy emotions could end up being dangerous, particularly since she had no real support network to catch her.

Shelley had to do something about that—and she wasn't about to let Zoe go home and wallow in it. Zoe could be intense at times. There was really no telling what she would do with that kind of emotion rolling around in her head, given that she didn't seem to have developed appropriate outlets for negative feelings. They just swum around, bottled up inside her. Maybe she was seeing a therapist now, but she had only been seeing them for a short while, and that wasn't enough yet to make a real difference.

"Why don't you come back and have dinner with me and my family, after we've finished up here?" Shelley asked, on instinct. That would get Zoe under her watchful eye, and might even cheer her up a little. There wasn't a lot that could stop a unicorn-obsessed toddler from putting a smile on someone's face, in Shelley's experience. She would call her husband from the car and let him know to put on a bigger meal. He never minded having company.

"Have dinner?" Zoe repeated. "While Dr. Applewhite sits in there, alone?"

Shelley tilted her head. It was funny how Zoe could be so disconnected at times. When she cared about someone, though, she cared about them deeply. To the bone. She had a loyalty that could not be questioned. It was one of the factors that made her endearing, even if other people didn't often see it. "Dr. Applewhite will sit in there, alone, whether you eat with me or not. Look, just come back with me, okay? I don't want you going home on your own tonight. You need some company."

"I do not wish to intrude on your family time."

The response was stiff, and most people might have taken it as rude. They might have thought that Zoe didn't care for, or want to meet, Shelley's family. But Shelley was seeing through that exterior, and she saw someone who was confused, tired, and carrying a heavy emotional burden. Someone who felt so guilty, she was starting to think she was bad for anyone to be around.

Shelley couldn't let her think that.

"You won't be intruding," Shelley said, smiling to prove it. She was going to look after Zoe, whether she wanted it or not. She needed looking after. She needed protecting from all the bad that was out there in the world, so much of which she had had to deal with already. It wasn't right for her to go home on her own. "I insist. Come on, Z, seriously. I'm not taking no for an answer. Get your things together. You can drive there behind me and go home after. I'll take care of the booking process."

Zoe sighed, and Shelley danced a victory dance inside her head. "Fine," Zoe said, her voice heavy with both reluctance and defeat. "I will meet you in the parking lot."

Zoe pulled up on the road outside a two-story home in a suburban neighborhood, noting the presence of sixteen miniature fence posts around a small front yard and the four windows, each fitted with white blinds. She also took in the two cars on the drive—no doubt necessary for Shelley and her husband to keep their respective careers, with Shelley's schedule being so unpredictable.

Zoe noted all of this and continued to look, because for as long as she was making observations, she wasn't getting out of the car. And the longer she could stay before getting out of the car, the longer it would be before small talk and socializing and the chaos of a household with a young child.

She sighed to herself and disengaged her seatbelt, knowing that she was being childish. She just didn't much feel like talking and laughing with a stranger when all she could think about was Dr. Applewhite, spending the night in a cell.

Shelley was waiting for her on a neatly manicured path that cut through the grass of the front lawn, her back to her own house. Zoe joined her, doing up the middle button on her suit jacket, trying to mentally steel herself for what was about to come.

"Don't look so worried," Shelley said, elbowing her gently in the ribs as they paused at the front door. "I'm not married to a dragon, and we aren't raising a werewolf. Just normal folks."

Zoe wasn't about to admit that normality was what she was afraid of, since it was so often completely alien to her. Nevertheless, she followed Shelley through the unlocked door, and entered a warm space that was instantly filled with the sounds of cooking emanating from the kitchen.

Zoe took a deep breath of the air, scenting herbs and vegetables against the rattling of pans and hum of an extractor fan above a steaming dish.

"I'm home," Shelley shouted at the top of her voice, making Zoe flinch.

She turned to see her colleague taking off her shoes and putting them onto a rack of five other pairs, and reluctantly did the same. Other people's customs at home—it was always strange to adapt to them. Zoe had two cats, and there seemed to be little point in sparing her carpets the touch of her shoes. They were already susceptible to loose fur, tracked mud, cat sick, and whatever small pieces of animal they had not quite finished eating after dragging them inside.

At least, when they could be bothered; Euler and Pythagoras were rather lazy in their middle age, seeming to prefer the tinned meats she brought them from the store.

"Mommy!"

A small whirlwind of pink rushed into the hall from another room and quickly collided with Shelley's legs. The young girl—who, Zoe remembered, was named Amelia—was quick on her feet, despite the fact that she must have been only just comfortable with walking and running. She held her hands up in the air for balance, until she could grasp onto her mother's calf for support.

"Hi, sweetie," Shelley said, leaning down to lift her daughter into her arms. "This is Mommy's friend, Zoe. Do you want to say hi?"

Amelia took one glance at Zoe and then hid, burying her head in her mother's shoulder.

Zoe watched with a growing sense of horror. Of course, the child would sense that there was something wrong with her. Children were intuitive. At least, normal children were. They knew when there was something off about a person. They knew it without being able to explain why.

Maybe Zoe should just excuse herself, back out, and go home. Her own mother's voice rang in her ears with that old familiar taunt: *devil child*.

"Don't be silly, you're not shy," Shelley chided with a laugh, bouncing Amelia up and down on her hip. "Come on. Say hello to Zoe."

Amelia turned back with a grin, her blonde hair brushing over her shoulders. "Hello!" she exclaimed, the word not quite fully formed, but distinguishable.

Zoe hesitated. What should she do? The girl looked happy enough, smiling and giggling. "... Hello, Amelia," she managed.

"Daddy's making dinner," Amelia announced proudly.

"It smells good," Zoe conceded.

Amelia, seemingly happy with the way the conversation had gone, laughed merrily and wiggled her feet. Shelley took this as a cue to put her down, and Amelia ran down the corridor toward the lights and sounds of the kitchen.

"You remembered," Shelley said, beaming.

For a second Zoe had no idea what she was talking about, until it dawned on her. "Of course. It is easy enough to remember your daughter's name."

"Not everyone does." Shelley squeezed Zoe's shoulder briefly, then followed her daughter down to the room that was mostly hidden past the doorway. Zoe could see that it extended to the right, but that was all. "Come on. Come meet Harry."

Harry was a new name, but Zoe assumed that it must refer to Shelley's husband—that was, of course, if they did not have a pet of any kind. Who else could it be?

She trailed behind Shelley, noting the presence of three framed photographs on the wall that each showed some variation of the family members in black and white, and into the kitchen. It opened up as she had predicted, some twenty feet along the whole of the back of the house, with an open-plan dining room on the other side. There were six chairs around the table, despite there being only three people in the family unit.

At the stovetop, there was a man standing with his back to them. He was six feet tall, and his back and shoulders were broad. He turned as they came in, brandishing a spatula that was coated in some kind of white sauce.

"Hey!" He grinned, as Shelley stepped forward to plant a kiss on his mouth. "You must be the famous Zoe."

Zoe watched their causal affection with growing jealousy. They were so comfortable, as if they barely even noticed the value of what they had. Zoe had never been close enough to anyone for those casual daily kisses that were as habitual as locking the door or brushing your hair. All of the relationships she had managed were short, and went nowhere. She had never so much as lived with another person since getting her first flat as a teen.

"Hello," she said, automatically, nodding a greeting. "It is nice to meet you."

"You, too," Harry said, turning back to his cooking while he talked over one shoulder. "I just love having guests over. I get to be a little more creative in the kitchen, you know?"

"You like to cook?" The green-eyed monster already stirring in Zoe's chest took another leap toward life. Not only was Shelley married with such a pretty child, but she had a husband who didn't mind taking on his share of work around the house?

"Well, with Shelley's hours, she wasn't always home to take care of it, so I learned. I have to say it's become a bit of a passion of mine. Me and Amelia take some time on the weekends to bake together, don't we, munchkin?"

Amelia giggled and joined her parents by the stove. "We made cookies," she said.

"That's right! We should have some after dinner. Z, you'll love them. We still have chocolate chip and oatmeal left," Shelley said, reaching to get down some half-full jars from a cupboard above the sink.

"That would be nice," Zoe said distantly, already feeling herself disengage from the conversation. She knew that she wasn't supposed to, but she was seeing that there were four cookies left in one jar but only three in the other, and that the cupboard contained seven other items before the door was closed, and that the joint on the door was slightly off by two degrees causing it to hang crooked, and everything was closing in on her.

Zoe didn't have this. She didn't have anything even close to this. She had one person in the world—just one. Not a parent, or a lover, or a child, but just one person that she could rely on and trust and always be comfortable with. Dr. Applewhite. And now she was in a cell at the FBI headquarters, waiting to go through further questioning in the morning rather than going home to her husband.

Dr. Applewhite's husband! How he must have been feeling! He would be so worried—and that was Dr. Applewhite's real family, wasn't it? Don was a lovely man, but he wasn't as close to Zoe as his wife was. He wouldn't see this from her side. He would be angry with Zoe. He would blame her, even if Dr. Applewhite didn't.

He would be right, too.

And here Zoe was, coming to the home of a colleague who was kind enough to show care for her at a difficult time—and what was she doing? Comparing herself, over and over, relentlessly. Studying Shelley's family and her home, judging her. Finding herself wanting. The flame of jealousy over Shelley's perfect life was twinned with one of shame, and it was all getting too much.

"I think it's about ready," Harry said. "I'll start dishing up. Amelia, honey, can you get some bowls out for me? You want to help Daddy serve dinner?"

Zoe wasn't supposed to be here. She didn't belong. She was intruding on this perfect picture, staining it just by being there. She wasn't the kind of good person that Shelley and Harry and Amelia were. She should have seen that from the beginning, should have stayed away.

She couldn't stay now.

"I have to go." She rushed out, turning abruptly and striding down the corridor.

There were fifteen steps to the door, and in the interim after her announcement there was a sudden silence in the kitchen. Then she heard the clattering of plates behind her, murmured yet hasty words from Shelley and Harry, and footsteps.

"Z, wait," Shelley called out, coming rapidly closer as Zoe grabbed her boots and started to put them back on. "Please, stay for dinner. It's cooked now. Just sit and eat, and you can go home right after."

"I cannot stay," Zoe told her, chancing a look up at her partner's face. She regretted it immediately. By the way a change came over Shelley's expression, Zoe gathered that she was showing too much of her inner turmoil on the outside.

Emotions were tricky. She wasn't good at faking the ones she did not feel, like everyone else was. But other people were good at hiding them, too, and Zoe had never been great at that. It was only when she had her ice-solid mask on, the lack of any kind of expression, that she had ever been able to fool anyone. It seemed that her mask must have slipped.

"Just take a breath, Z. Please. I know you're having a hard time right now, but that's what I'm here for. We're partners, right?"

Zoe, her boots now firmly in place, could not look at her. "Not here. Here you are a wife, a mother. I should not be here. I have to go."

She turned away from Shelley's pleading arms, opened the door, and strode away, unlocking her car as she went. She started the car without looking back and drove home, somehow not at all comforted by the thought of the microwave meal waiting for her along with her cats.

Chapter Twenty

Zoe watched a streetlight flickering up ahead at the end of the block, at the intersection with the next road along. On, off, on, off, on. The pattern appeared random, but of course, it wasn't. It was defined by the dying bulb inside it, or perhaps the flow of electricity in some damaged part of the light, or some other factor that Zoe was not aware of. If she had been an electrical engineer, perhaps she would even have been able to tell just by looking at it.

Of course, she was not an electrical engineer. As she walked an unfamiliar part of her neighborhood, her hands stuffed deep in the pockets of her coat and her breath clouding misty in the air, Zoe mused that it would have been an easier job. Fewer people to deal with.

She was not sure exactly where she was going, except for the fact that it had to be somewhere. Within half an hour of sitting at home, during which time she had managed only half a meal before starting to feel queasy, Zoe had become restless. Staying there was perhaps not as uncomfortable as staying at Shelley's, but it still didn't feel right. She had put on her coat and walked out the door, with no destination in mind.

The only thing she could focus on was Dr. Applewhite. Scenes played out in her mind, the two of them together. All of the many memories that they had shared over the years. Never once had Dr. Applewhite let her down or made her feel judged.

She was the one who had helped Zoe start to see her abilities as something useful, rather than an evil curse. Even if Zoe had never yet really been able to embrace them, much less be proud of them, they had become something that she was able to use. She saved lives now. She stopped people from killing, minimized risk, foiled escape plans. She stopped innocent people from being targeted for crimes that they did not commit.

Usually, anyway.

The worst part of all of this was that Dr. Applewhite had been the very person to set her on this path, to help her settle on law enforcement as a career. To encourage her to develop and nurture those skills, make use of them. How wrong of her it had been to think that this was the ideal solution! She was likely regretting it now, Zoe figured. Sitting alone in that cell at the J. Edgar Hoover building. Maybe she was awake like Zoe, unable to get comfortable in an unfamiliar place.

Zoe remembered being young and isolated, a college student with no idea of what to do with her life or where to go. Studying almost aimlessly, just picking up credits wherever she could with no real thought of what they would mean to her future life. She remembered taking a meeting with Dr. Applewhite, when everything had changed.

"Have you thought about what career you want to pursue?" Dr. Applewhite asked, as she moved a pawn across the chessboard between them.

Zoe studied the board intently. She had no real interest in the game, but the challenge was to try and identify possible strategies. The numbers she could see on the board told her where each of Dr. Applewhite's pieces could go next, how many moves it would take her to get close to the queen. How many of them were mathematically placed for a check, and how she could avoid those moves.

"No," Zoe said bluntly. She had been even more blunt back then, though no one who knew her now would likely believe it.

Dr. Applewhite moved another pawn, though Zoe sensed her mind wasn't fully in it. If it was, then she would not have made such an obvious move. "I think it's important for you to find a sense of purpose in what you do. Have you considered a career where you might help people?"

Zoe glanced up, frowning. "Like medicine? I don't know. I think you need to have more compassion for that."

Dr. Applewhite's lips quirked at the edges, a trait that Zoe found annoying. What did it even mean? "I don't know about that. I've met plenty of nurses who don't seem to care about much of anything," Dr. Applewhite said. "And you're plenty compassionate. But there are other options. What about law enforcement?"

Zoe was about to offer a verbal rebuttal alongside the one on the game board, but her hand hovered in midair. That was a striking thought. Law enforcement. What if she could use her pattern recognition, her calculations, all of it, to identify suspects and stop crime sprees?

What if she could stop murders?

"Like the police?"

Dr. Applewhite nodded. "Police, FBI, whatever you want. There are a lot of options around here, and you could move to another state, too. Go be a small-town sheriff if you wanted, or head up a specialist investigation unit. There's even the forensics department, CSI. It seems like it's worth considering."

Zoe did consider it. She considered it long and hard. So long that their time together was up before the chess game was finished.

Zoe's mother had always called her evil. Said the devil's blood must run in her veins in order for her to do the things she did. Zoe knew that was stupid, because her father was just a man, and her mother was human too—for all her shortcomings. But if she could help people, really help people . . . if she could put the real bad guys behind bars, wouldn't that change things?

Wouldn't that redeem her, just a little?

The irony stung. Redeem herself? Ha! Not only had she failed to protect an innocent person in this case, but it was the very person who had suggested she make a career out of it in the first place.

The case was a mess. Zoe had had no leads before she implicated Dr. Applewhite, and she had none now. In fact, the only lead that could really be called credible in the whole case was the DNA evidence—and that was what had gotten Dr. Applewhite pulled in.

Zoe felt useless. There was nowhere for her to go on the case, no lead to follow. She had no idea where to start looking for this killer, now that the equations hadn't panned out the way she thought they would. It was clearly a frame, but Dr. Applewhite came across hundreds of people on a weekly basis. How could they narrow down thousands of people to just one suspect, when Dr. Applewhite wasn't the type to make enemies?

It wasn't like she had anyone else who could help either. Besides Shelley, no one knew about the numbers that she could see. Until the forensics people finally caught on to what she already knew—the height of the perpetrator—there was nothing at all to say that Dr. Applewhite wasn't guilty. And Shelley just had to be the person that Zoe, in her infinite wisdom, had pushed away tonight.

Not only had she made a mess in the first place, but now it was messed up even more.

Zoe felt something wet drip down from her chin, and was startled to realize that she was crying. It was not often that she engaged in such an outward show of emotion like this, least of all a negative one. She tried to remember the last time that she had cried, and couldn't. The shock of it caught her breath in her throat, froze the water in her eyes. She wiped her face dry with her sleeve, biting her lip until the impulse went away entirely.

There was something she could do here. There had to be. There was something she had missed, somewhere, and all she had to do was find it.

She ran through all three of the equations, by now learned by heart. They still didn't make sense, but what if she inverted them? Reversed them? What if she substituted the letters so that all of the equations matched? What if she tried numbers one by one, looked for a solution?

Maybe solving them at last would spell something out, like geographical coordinates. Of course, for that she would need to have the inputs, and she had no idea what c or d or f was supposed to represent.

Something to do with the college maybe?

And the victims themselves—they had to have more to reveal, they had to. Zoe went over the crime scene photographs that she had burned into her memory again, trying to see them in as much detail as possible. Five foot nine, yes, it had to be, and more than one hundred and thirty-five pounds. But how much more? Could she set an upper limit? The perpetrator would not be obese, because they were fit enough to attack and to get away without leaving behind weighted impressions in the ground.

There was something, somewhere, in all of this. There had to be.

If there wasn't, Zoe was never going to forgive herself.

A buzz from her pocket brought her back to the real world, and she looked down at her phone to see a message alert. It was from John—the man she had seen for just a single date, and who both Dr. Monk and Dr. Applewhite seemed positive she should see again.

What a moment for him to reach out to her.

Hey, Zoe. How are you? I was wondering if you wanted to meet up for a drink?—John

Zoe didn't need to read this one three times, or leave it until the morning to decide, or turn to her therapist for advice. She knew what she wanted to say. John had been trying for a long time, and it was time that paid off for him. She wrote back and sent it immediately, not hesitating to consider whether she was doing the right thing.

Yes. Are you available right now?

Chapter Twenty One

The cocktail bar was crowded, but Zoe tried to ignore the mass of bodies dotted around the tables and focus on moving through them. She was bad with crowds at the best of times—too much to see and notice—but John had already texted her to let her know that he was sitting near the window. She just had to get over there.

Had to get through the one-foot gap which narrowed to half a foot where one man had pushed his chair out too far, past the four couples and the three groups, past seventeen glasses on tables. The staff was efficient—no empty glasses left to sit as superfluous. That was a positive sign, at least.

She couldn't quite see him in the dim lighting until she drew closer, training her steps as close to the glass as possible so that she could effectively blank out most of the room behind her. Then she recognized him—at first by his shape, the same height and bulk as she remembered, and then by the facial features lit by the glow of a small candle on the table. The song playing in the background, under the chatter of those around them, was four beats per bar. Three chords. Simple and inoffensive.

"Zoe," he said, standing up from his chair as she approached. A little old-fashioned. "You made it!"

He sounded genuinely surprised. Zoe felt a stab of guilt at that. She supposed that she had not been efficient at returning his messages. "John, hello. It is good to see you again."

John waited for her to sit before he did. "You look wonderful."

"Thank you." Zoe was too busy thinking about the fact that she had not dressed up and did not, in fact, look wonderful. It was only when a brief flicker passed over his expression that she remembered: most people liked to have a compliment returned, and she should have politely remarked that he looked good, as well. Such things had always seemed stupid to her. How could one ever think a compliment was genuine, if it was enforced by courtesy?

"I ordered you a martini. I hope you don't mind," John said, hastily continuing with many a waved hand gesture. He was wearing a white shirt today. Last time, it had been blue with two-millimeter stripes. "If you don't like it, I'll drink it. I just thought I'd better get something for you if I was ordering for myself. I figured you wouldn't be long."

He was talking a lot. More than last time, maybe. His rate of words per minute was higher, which normally indicated nervousness. Or fear. "Thank you," Zoe said again, wondering if she was going to be able to get any more words in edgewise. "I will drink it."

In truth, she did not drink often. Did she like martinis? She couldn't even recall. It was a rare occasion that she touched alcohol, mostly because she didn't like that weird, wavy, out-of-control feeling that everyone else seemed to relish. When the room began to sway and all the numbers got wonky and out of sync. Depth perception, sense of direction, mathematical ability, all of it began to disappear the more alcohol she had. It wasn't a pleasant sensation.

But tonight, maybe it would be good to get detached from everything a little. To drown out the horrible things she couldn't help thinking about herself.

"I didn't think you were going to get back to me," John admitted, picking up his own glass. It was considerably more masculine than the one prepared for her: a tumbler filled with amber liquid, not a recipe that Zoe could name. She couldn't find a justification for taking up space in her memory with knowledge about cocktails.

"I have been busy lately." It was only partly true. Yes, Zoe had been busy with caseloads, paperwork, court cases. But she was always busy with those things. She had been busy when she was talking to him on the dating site in the first place. It was her own personal doubt that had led her to avoid his messages.

"I know the feeling." John smiled briefly. His lips curved higher on the right than on the left. Oh, yes, that was right: he was a lawyer. "Anything you can talk about? I know these cases are often pretty hush-hush before they get to court."

Zoe inclined her head, grateful for the out. "Sadly, they are all awaiting trial." It wasn't quite true. Her and Shelley's last big case, the Golden Ratio killer, had been dead even before they prevented his final crime. There was never going to be any trial for him. They had proven beyond a doubt that he was guilty, and that was enough.

But Zoe didn't want to talk about that. Not now, when she had something bigger on her mind. Besides, it was done and buried. There wasn't a lot of point in retracing the past.

She sipped her martini, feeling the unfamiliar burn of alcohol down her throat. She saw the size in inches of the olive before she closed her eyes briefly, to shut it out, and put the offending object in her mouth. No numbers tonight, please, she thought. If only she could turn them off. Stop them from flashing up everywhere she looked.

When she opened her eyes again, John was looking at her with an odd expression. "Bad day?" he asked.

Ah. That expression was sympathy. "Difficult case," Zoe said, and shrugged. "I do not want to talk about it."

John paused, then nodded. His hair, a light brown cropped short, gleamed with the sheen of good conditioning in the light as his head moved. "All right. Well, this will cheer you up. A funny story about a client of mine. So, we were there in the courtroom, waiting for the judge, and everyone started getting restless. This judge, he's usually punctual. I mean, they all are as a rule."

Zoe lost herself in John's story, trying to listen just to his words, look just at his face. If she focused really hard, she could block everything else out. For a brief moment she felt no guilt anymore, before it slipped back in again. A moment's relief was a start. She fought to get that control back, to exist only in the flow of John's voice and the slide of the martini down her throat.

"So we're wondering what the hell is going on. Time passes, another few minutes, and he bursts in. Come to find out some secretary or something had made an error in the courtroom schedule. All the cases got assigned times, but on the judge's copy of the schedule, it was half an hour later. He was furious—absolutely raving. Not great for the defense, but for us, it was a great start," John continued.

She wasn't used to drinking at all, and she had forgotten how it could change her. She could feel it running through her body like a current in her veins, making her feel strange, not herself. That, in itself, was welcome.

"The defense, he's just a public defender. Not a great court record. The guy has a hundred different files spilling out of his briefcase, stuff for the next eight or ten cases he has to appear in. He's worked like a dog. Barely has any idea where he is. So the first thing he does is he gets the defendant's name wrong. Then he calls the judge by the wrong name. I lean over in a quiet moment and I say to him, maybe we'd better ask for adjournment? You know, let him get up to speed a bit better.

"But he's cocky, arrogant type. I don't think he wants to have to come back to this client, either. The guy is practically foaming at the mouth, and so is the judge. Soon enough we start hearing evidence and the defendant is shouting out—screaming every few minutes. Refuting things, calling people names. Judge keeps on warning him. I'm looking at the public defender like, come on, buddy. Let's call it a day, huh? Let me give you a lifeline. But he's adamant. He wants to press on.

"Next up the defendant suddenly stands up and says this is all bullcrap and he's not standing for it anymore, and he wants to see a real judge. The judge gets mad—like you've never seen mad before. Steam coming out of his ears. And he asks the defendant if he has the receipt—the receipt to say that his purchase on the land went through, you see. Proof that he paid it out of his bank account or that my client ever received it, anything to show he had ownership. And the guy stands there and splutters and says no, he didn't bring it.

"And so the judge ended up throwing the case out. Can you believe that?"

Zoe laughed at the appropriate moment, not because it was what normal people did but because the story had actually been funny. "I cannot believe that the public defender did not follow your advice. He must have been some idiot, after all that."

"Yeah, well, we do get them," John laughed, finishing his drink. He was clean-shaven, but there was a spot just under the bend of his jaw on the left that he had missed, a tiny piece of stubble. "I bet you get a lot of that in your line of work, too. Idiots, I mean."

"You could say that. Although I have been known to think they are the people who work alongside me, not the people we arrest, at times."

"Ouch," John said, but he was grinning. "Office politics?"

"Something like that." Zoe would normally stop there, but something made her want to go on. Maybe it was John's wonderful narrative skills brushing off on her. "I have a hard time keeping a partner. I am not great at not telling people what I think of them to their face, and apparently you are not supposed to do that in the workplace."

John's eyebrow quirked. "Oh, dear. Am I about to find out what you really think of me?"

Zoe waved a hand. "I have not known you long enough yet to form a fair assessment, but I am of the opinion that you are an excellent storyteller, at least."

"That's good to know." John took a handful of nuts out of a small dish in the middle of the table and started crunching his way through them. His arms muscles flexed. Zoe had already noted previously that he must have been a regular gym-goer. "So, what's your partner like at the moment? Is he hard to get on with?"

"She," Zoe corrected, then shook her head thoughtfully. "Actually, I get on with Shelley better than with anyone else so far. She is not an idiot. She is a lot quicker than I gave her credit for at first, even. And she has such a perfect little family. Really. She is a wonderful person."

John made a face. "She sounds boring."

Zoe laughed briefly. "Fortunately she's not. She can be fierce at times, too. In short, she is a far better agent than I am."

"But you're smarter than her."

Zoe cocked her head. "I did not say that."

"You didn't need to." John tossed back another nut and swallowed it before continuing with a twinkle in his eye. "I can tell. You're the smartest person in any given room you walk into, aren't you?"

Zoe flushed a little. "I would not . . . I mean . . ."

John waved a hand. "Don't be modest. Anyway, tell me about this case. Something's happened between you and your partner that you don't know how to deal with, right?"

"You are perceptive."

"You're talking about this woman like she's the best thing since sliced bread, but you're obviously struggling in some kind of way. Or you wouldn't have accepted my invitation." Zoe opened her mouth to protest, but John cut her off with a short shake of his head. "It's okay. I don't mind how I get you here, so long as I can charm you while I've got you. That way I might have a shot at date number three. So, what's the problem?"

Zoe hesitated. There were a lot of things here that she could not talk about, not without getting into trouble. But there were things that were already in the papers—things that other people would already know.

"Did you hear about the killings on campus this past week?"

John's eyes widened and his eyebrows shot up. "That's your case?"

"Yes. And we have a suspect in custody." Zoe drew in a heavy breath. "Unfortunately, not only am I sure beyond a shadow of a doubt that this suspect is innocent, but I also have a close personal connection with them. Which means..."

"Which means that no one is going to take your word for it, because they assume that you're too close to see the big picture." John shook his head. "That sucks. Listen, do you want another drink?"

Zoe paused, thinking about how the martini was already swimming in her system. "I will take a soda."

She was expecting pushback, but John nodded respectively and got up. "School night—no heavy drinking. Got it. I'll be right back."

When John returned, Zoe was quite surprised to find that she had been waiting for him. That she was eager, indeed, to tell him more.

Perhaps John's skill was not just in telling stories, but also in listening to them, because she did tell him more. She told him all about Dr. Applewhite, minus a few details—like her name, the exact nature of the evidence against her, and the diagnosis that she had helped bring about. She even ended up telling him about getting emancipation from her mother as a teen, about how she had supported herself for a long time. And when she was done with that, she circled back around to her original point, and the equations—which had been mentioned openly in the press—that she was trying to solve.

It was only when she finished this part of the story, and looked up to see that the bar was almost deserted, that Zoe realized she must have been talking for quite some time.

"Oh, I am sorry," she said, embarrassed suddenly by her loquaciousness. "You must be tired of hearing me talk by now."

"Not at all," John said, and the fact that he didn't even smile when he said it made her more inclined to believe that he wasn't just being nice. "All of this has been... fascinating. I mean, your job is so much more high-stakes than mine. Not to mention everything that you've been through... I can't imagine coming out of that as strong as you are."

This time, Zoe knew that her cheeks were heating up. "I am just—average," she said, even though she knew that was the one thing she really wasn't. "I do not think I am special just for how I grew up. Everyone goes through some kind of adversity."

"But you're brilliant." John reached out across the table and touched her hand, and there was a hint of laughter on his face—one that she could not interpret. "Wow. I mean, I wanted to see you again after the first date. But this . . . you were holding out on me. Seriously, I'm blown away by how brilliant you are."

Zoe barely knew how to reply to that. Most men were not so complimentary, and when they were she would sense that it was not genuine. But John really seemed to mean what he was saying, at least according to her limited ability to tell.

There was another chord that his words struck, however, and it was not a pleasant one. "If I was so brilliant, I would have figured out what the equations mean already." She sighed, toying with her empty glass. "But I have nothing. Just a jumbled mess."

"Hey, you'll get there," John was saying, but Zoe's concentration was drifting away from him. She sat up straighter, frowning a little. *Jumbled mess* . . . why did that sound so . . . right?

Jumbled mess . . . what was it that James Wardenford had told her, when she had him in for questioning?

Something's wrong. It's like all of the elements are there, but they've been placed incorrectly. Imbalanced. Too much on one side, not enough on the other.

Imbalanced. Placed incorrectly.

There was something here . . .

"Zoe?"

Zoe frowned at the unwelcome interruption, shaking her head quickly and throwing her hand up in the air to indicate that silence was needed. Her brain was a little slow, still coping with the effects of the alcohol.

Everything was there. The equations had been written out in full, but they didn't work. Nothing was missing—no extra parts hidden anywhere on the bodies, no missed signs. She had seen that for herself when they found Edwin North.

If there was nothing more to add, that meant that they already had all of the pieces of the puzzle. Zoe had tried to make sense of them by cutting bits out and putting them together, like some kind of mega-equation birthed from the incorrect parts. But that still left the lines she had not included, and the ones that were put together pointed in the wrong direction. Toward an innocent person.

Which meant that she still didn't have them in the right order.

Edwin North had been able to afford his grand Georgian colonial because he was a neurologist. Not a professor or a student. He had no real connection with the college, but the cause of death seemed to tie him to the others—not to mention the equation scrawled across his chest. They had been mentioned in the papers, but not printed in full. The only person who would know enough about the other equations to finish off the clue pointing to Dr. Applewhite had to be the killer.

Ergo, there had to be a reason why the killer had stepped outside of the college in order to target a seemingly unrelated neurologist.

And what did neurologists deal with? The brain. The brain, which, when it went wrong—like hers did when she consumed alcohol—could mess things up. Jumble them around.

This was it. This was the breakthrough that Zoe had been waiting for.

She snatched her phone up from the table and dialed Shelley's number from her call list, hoping she wasn't asleep or screening her calls. Zoe wouldn't blame her, after what had happened earlier, but Shelley answered after only a couple of rings.

"Z? Are you all right? I've been worried about you. I tried to call you, but—"

"I am sorry about earlier. But I need you to listen now." Zoe tried to keep the distractions to a minimum, hoping that Shelley would be impressed with the importance of what she was saying enough to stop focusing on the past. "I have had a breakthrough. Meet me at the hospital where Edwin North worked as soon as you can. We need to check some patient records."

"What? Zoe, what have you found?"

Zoe put the phone down without answering. They could talk as they walked through the hospital corridors to where they needed to be. Discussing it now wasn't going to get them there any quicker.

Zoe returned her attention to John, who was looking at her with a slightly open-mouthed expression. She glanced at his glass and realized he had made the gesture of switching to soft drinks along with her. "I am not used to drinking, and it goes to my head too much," she said, by way of explanation. "Did you drive here?"

John nodded silently, reaching into his pocket to draw out a set of car keys.

"Good. I need you to drive me to the hospital—and we need to go now."

Chapter Twenty Two

Zoe let go of her seatbelt and breathed out slowly, trying to re-center herself.

"Sorry," John said. "I tried to drive smoothly, but it sounded like time was of the essence."

"It was," Zoe said, opening the passenger's side door. "It is. I get carsick no matter what. Thank you for the ride."

She got out and shut the door behind her, her obligations of politeness toward John now completely forgotten. There was something more pressing to think about: figuring out who the serial killer stalking Georgetown really was, and clearing Dr. Applewhite's name.

Zoe strode across smooth flooring laid out in predictable tile patterns, upset at ugly points by the placement of a chair or a desk in an inappropriate place that messed up the lines, passing the waiting area without seeing Shelley. Her home was much farther away than the cocktail bar had been. Zoe figured she wouldn't arrive for a while yet. There was no time to sit around and wait for her.

"Neurology department?" she barked at the reception desk. She had been in enough hospitals across the country, visiting victims and taking statements, to know that they were often mazelike and impossible to predict unless you knew the entire history of the building. Maybe it made sense that cardiology should be next to the pediatric ward if you knew that the departments had received funding one after the other for new extensions to the building, but no sane person would have built them like that on purpose. It didn't help that the plane symmetry was thrown off by refurbishments that cut across old tiles, hurting Zoe's eyes and making it all the more confusing.

The woman behind the desk was, like almost all receptionists Zoe had ever come across, slow and supercilious. On top of that, she had to weigh a hundred and eighty-five pounds, and she was pushing sixty. She raised eyebrows from behind glasses slid low on her nose, and looked Zoe up and down. "Are you a patient or a visitor?"

"Neither. Where is it?" Zoe hated moments like this, the delay of small-minded people. There seemed to be so many of them in the world, totally unfazed by the concept of efficiency or practicality.

"If you are a patient, you have to sign in at the touchscreen here and wait for your name to be called before you go the neurology department," the receptionist was saying, pointing a lazy, fat wrist in the direction of the device. "If you are a visitor, you need to collect a visitor's pass and give the name of the person you are here to see. Visiting hours are over, however, so visitor's passes are not currently available. If you are neither of those things, you will have to leave this hospital."

Zoe rolled her eyes and yanked her badge out of her pocket, slamming it down on the desk in front of the receptionist. "I can go wherever I like in this hospital," she hissed, delivering a glower that she hoped would do the desired job of making this woman do her damn job. "Now, tell me the quickest way to get to the neurology department."

The receptionist made a show of studying the badge, lifting her glasses up by the arm to push them closer to her eyes as she squinted. "Well, Agent," she began, as slow as was humanly possible, "you first take the second right, then you will need to go up in the elevator to the third floor. Turn left twice at your earliest opportunities, and then take the third right, and you will be at the neurology waiting area."

Zoe snatched her badge back, already beginning to turn away. "Another special agent is coming. Tell her where to find me," she shot over her shoulder, not bothering to wait to see if the woman would agree.

She would agree, or Zoe would have her up on charges of obstructing justice. She was not in the mood to be messed around with today.

The directions might have been confusing for someone who did not easily grasp patterns and numbers, but Zoe had laid out a miniature map in her mind even as the woman was speaking. Ignore the first right, then turn, then up and up. She tapped her foot restlessly as the elevator traveled slowly and smoothly, designed not to be uncomfortable for those in need of medical attention. A doctor in whites and two other visitors eyed her strangely, no doubt picking up on her impatience. Now that Zoe had the answer within her grasp, she wanted it as soon as possible. She wanted it five minutes ago. All of this had to end, and now.

The elevator dinged, the doors slid open, and Zoe was shouldering her way out of them almost before there was enough room for her to get through. Left, left, skip two and then right—and there it was. A small and modest sign printed on blue plastic hung above the doorway, declaring this to be the Neurology Department.

And below it, just beyond the doors, another reception desk—with another woman approaching retirement age, another victim of a few too many donuts.

Zoe felt her heart sink, but she pressed on. At least there was someone to talk to. She would need to talk to someone, after all, if she was going to get her hands on the patient records.

This time, she did not waste minutes asking questions that were not going to be answered. She lifted her badge as she approached and then placed it down on the desk in case the woman would want to examine it. "Special Agent Zoe Prime. I need to see this department's patient records. What kind of search functions do you have available on your database?"

The receptionist stared at her and blinked. Her hair was tinged gray at the very top only. She must have dyed the rest, maybe recently made a decision to stop and let it grow out. She glanced down and read the badge, verifying that it was real, before looking up expectantly. "May I see the warrant?"

Zoe paused.

Ah.

The one thing she did not have.

Truth be told, she had let all thoughts of procedure fly out of her head. Call it a side effect of the alcohol, call it sheer excitement at the thought that she might be able to clear Dr. Applewhite. Whatever it was, she had only thought about reading the records themselves—not about how she was going to do that.

"There is no time to get a warrant. This is extremely urgent. I need to find a person fitting a particular neurological profile."

The receptionist narrowed her eyes and leaned back in her chair, folding her arms across her chest. "You mean to tell me that you don't even have a warrant?"

Zoe didn't need to have the ability to read nuance and subtlety of tone and gesture to know that this was not going well. "This is extremely important. You have heard of the murders on campus?"

"I heard about them," the receptionist agreed, shrugging her meaty shoulders up and down. "But I can't help you, sister. You need to come back when you have a warrant. That's how the law works."

Zoe covered her face with her hands for a moment, trying to think of a way to explain this to the woman without biting her head off. "Look, you do not understand."

"I understand fine enough." The receptionist shook her head resolutely, turning her attention back to her computer screen. "No warrant, no access."

"Zoe?"

Zoe turned, grateful to see Shelley approaching them fast. Her hair was slightly mussed, her makeup not quite as neat as usual. Zoe figured Shelley must have already been getting ready for bed when she called.

"She will not let me see the records," Zoe said, setting her mouth in a firm line of displeasure.

"Without a warrant, right?" Shelley nodded, looking between Zoe and the receptionist as she arrived next to them. She took a breath, perhaps assessing the situation, before continuing. "May I speak with the administrator? Just to discuss further. We might need to schedule a visit."

"No, we need to see the records now," Zoe hissed, trying to get Shelley's attention.

Shelley looked up at her, giving her an odd tilt of the head and raise of the eyebrows that Zoe could not decipher. "Let's just talk to the administrator and see what's possible. At least that way we can expedite the process."

The receptionist made a face, eyebrows high and eyes sliding off to the side. "I'll give him a call. But I would be surprised if he's still in this late."

The phone rang for eight seconds before someone on the other end answered. The receptionist could not contain the shock on her face as she spoke to them, explaining the situation. Zoe did not even try to contain her own spiteful glee when she put the receiver down and invited them to wait in the chairs provided.

The eleven minutes it took for the administrator to arrive were almost interminable. Zoe was so hopped up on the energy of maybe getting this all solved that she could barely sit still. She checked her phone for messages, her emails, examined the magazines scattered on a low side table, read every piece of literature and every poster dotted around the room. Shelley was calm and still, and though she must have been curious, she didn't ask. Not while the receptionist was there in the room, listening.

A man in his mid-fifties came to the desk and quickly after looked their way. He was six feet tall, perhaps a fraction of an inch over. Then again, that could have been the soles of his shoes. He was thin and dressed in a sharp brown suit with a blue shirt and tie bearing half-inch-thick darker blue stripes.

"Agents?" he said, stepping forward with an outstretched hand.

"I'm Special Agent Shelley Rose, and this is my colleague, Special Agent Zoe Prime," Shelley said, shaking his hand first and then pausing for Zoe to do the same. "It's good of you to come and speak with us. I appreciate that it's late."

"No, no, not to worry at all," he said. "I'm Gary Burke. I've just left a meeting with the hospital board, so I was still here anyway."

"All the same." Shelley smiled. "May we speak with you in a private room?"

"Of course." Burke gestured toward an unmarked door off to the side. "Please, follow me in here. We won't be disturbed."

The room was small, but comfortable enough for the three of them. It contained just five chairs and a water machine, as well as a drooping houseplant. No doubt it was set aside for those who needed a little more privacy while they waited.

"So, ladies, how may I help you?" Burke asked, with the door closed firmly behind them.

"It's a little delicate," Shelley began. "You see, we're investigating a very serious case. The details need to be kept quiet from the press, inasmuch as we can. Several murders have been reported this week, and we believe we're very close to our suspect."

"The deaths on the campus?" Burke guessed.

"And your colleague, too. Dr. Edwin North."

Burke's mouth gaped open, and his face paled. "They're connected? Of course, I had heard about the tragic loss, but—you're saying this is the same case?"

"I'm afraid so, Mr. Burke, but if you could keep that between us, it would be appreciated."

"Of course, of course. Please—just Gary is fine."

Zoe watched with a kind of frenzied detachment. She wanted so badly for this conversation to be over so that they could get on with really looking, checking the records and finding what they needed. It was always like watching a miracle be performed, seeing Shelley work people over. Zoe couldn't tell if it was the words she used, the expressions, the body language, or just that she had a much prettier face, but somehow, she was always able to win them over.

It was really only a matter of time. Burke might have worked with neurosurgeons, but he wasn't one himself. Zoe stayed quiet, knowing that the only thing she could contribute here would be to mess it up.

"Gary, right. It's clear to us that the same perpetrator is behind all of the attacks, and your Dr. North is actually the missing link we've been looking for. We need to check his patient records, to find anyone who fits the bill so that we can track them down."

"Oh, I see—yes, well, that shouldn't be a problem," Burke said. "I'll just need to take a copy of the warrant for our own records."

Shelley bit her lip and made a face. "See, that's where it gets really delicate," Shelley said. "We haven't had the time to get in front of a judge, and we won't be able to until tomorrow. We're chasing a hot lead here. If we wait until the morning and come back, by the time we have that paperwork, the killer could be long gone."

Burke hesitated, his composure faltering. "Well—you see—I-I'm not really supposed to allow you access to anything without a warrant. No one outside of the hospital staff, actually."

"No, I completely understand that," Shelley said. "And we wouldn't want you to lose your job or get into trouble. We won't ask you to let us see the records right now."

Zoe shot her a look. They wouldn't?

"There is, however, a way around this. A way we can get justice for Dr. North and stop this killer from striking again, without breaking any of the rules," Shelley went on.

Burke cleared his throat. "What did you have in mind?"

"You look at the records. We can give you the parameters, tell you what we're looking for. All we need from you is a name." Shelley smiled sweetly, spreading her hands in front of her as if to demonstrate how easy it would all be. "Tomorrow, once we have him locked up where he can't hurt anyone else, we come back with a warrant to check the records and make official copies. That way it's all sewn up."

Burke looked a little unsure, but he cleared his throat again. "I suppose—for Dr. North," he suggested.

"Yes. In his memory," Shelley nodded.

"All right." Burke sighed and squared his shoulders. "What am I looking for?"

Shelley turned to Zoe, who now understood that was her cue. "A recent diagnosis of dyslexia," she said. "I can tell you that the man will be around five foot nine and one hundred and thirty-five pounds or more, but we can also consider cases that fall slightly below those figures. It should be in the last six months—most likely even the last three or four."

"All right, I'll input that," Burke replied. "Those figures—you're expecting an adult?"

"An adult or a teen, college age," Zoe supplied, a thought coming to her. "Oh—and dyscalculia as well. Or aphasia. Anything that would cause difficulties with written communication."

"That widens the field considerably," Burke said, but he was smiling. "I can't check the records of any other site, of course, but I can tell you if he treated someone here. I'll be back in two shakes, ladies. Wait here for me."

When the door was closed behind him, Shelley sat on one of the vacant chairs, much of the pasted-on pleasantness disappearing as she dropped. "Wow. I was just about to go to sleep, and you suddenly cracked the case."

"Sorry," Zoe said.

"I wasn't complaining. So, written communication? You found something in the numbers?"

"I was reminded of something Wardenford said—that it was all out of order, jumbled up. The more I thought about that, the more sense it made. I do not think the killer knows that they are jumbled—or at least, if he does, he is not able to fix it. Neurological damage could also account for a sudden outburst of violence."

"Dyslexia isn't something I normally associate with violent outbursts," Shelley said, quirking the corners of her lips.

"No, but it does not always appear . . . out of nowhere. That is the wrong term, but you can see what I mean: it does not always develop during the process of one's early life. That is to say, brain injuries or tumors, or so on, can cause other neurological difficulties to appear."

"And they can also cause changes in behavior, such as violent mood swings," Shelley nodded. "Got it."

"When we have his name, we should move immediately. We do not know if he is planning another attack. Granted, the existing victims appear to perfectly spell out Dr. Applewhite's equation as a clue for us to chase after, but that may not be the final piece of his puzzle."

"That's another thing, we'll need to verify that she knows him in some way. Or that he could access the equation somehow. I gather it wasn't widely shared, so that will be another piece of evidence against him they can use in court."

Zoe nodded. "After we have had that confirmed, we can let her go home."

Shelley smiled at her, looking tired in that moment. Before they could say anything more, the door opened and Burke returned.

He was hesitant, pausing a few seconds and wetting his lips without saying anything.

"Well?" Zoe asked, impatient. Did he not realize how costly a delay could be? "What is his name?"

"That's the thing," Burke said, clasping his hands together. Hands that were conspicuously empty of any kind of printout or note. "There aren't any patients on file that fit the criteria you mentioned."

Zoe stared at him, her mouth open. How could this be? Had she made a huge mistake?

Chapter Twenty Three

Zoe stood in the almost empty reception area, looking at the patients sitting and waiting to see doctors without really seeing them. Even at this time of night, there were people around—referred from the ER, perhaps, or scheduled for late-night procedures because the operating suites were otherwise full.

"We just have to keep working on it. It was a good theory, but we'll come up with another one," Shelley said. "Who knows? Maybe you're right, but this person hasn't actually had a diagnosis yet."

"But Dr. North," Zoe said helplessly. "There had to be a reason why he was connected to all of this."

"I know it made a lot of sense. We'll have to come at it from another angle. Maybe he knew one of the other victims in a way we haven't put together yet." Shelley reached out to squeeze Zoe's upper arm, then checked her watch and sighed. "In the morning, anyway. I'm going home to get a few hours of sleep. You should, too."

Zoe nodded, though that wasn't exactly an agreement. She wasn't sure just yet that she wanted to lock herself into any decisions.

She watched Shelley leave, then pushed herself into action, trailing after her. It was not until Shelley had disappeared out through the wide automatic doors and into the night that Zoe remembered how she had arrived here—and that she therefore did not have a vehicle of her own in the parking lot.

She sighed to herself. She should have asked Shelley to drive her home. Now it was going to be a very expensive cab ride, all because she had been too busy trying to work out how she could possibly have been wrong.

But, really, how could she? It had all made the most perfect sense. Dr. North, targeted because he made the diagnosis. A new brain deficiency partnered with a new level of rage and violence, turning a misplaced anger into a murderous impulse. The equations, left as a message but somehow bungled by a man who could no longer make them work. A mathematician. Someone who would have known both of the other victims from Georgetown.

It all fit so perfectly! Zoe thought about going back and checking that Burke had considered other possibilities, like brain tumors, but she stopped herself. She had been clear—anything that could cause difficulties with written communication. The man worked in a hospital. He would know to check for anything fitting those signs.

Zoe stepped out into the cool night air, grateful for the way that it soothed her head and the aching tension she had barely noticed was building there. She was about to call for a taxi when her eyes drifted left, and she saw him.

John—sitting on a bench just over from the entrance, now lifting a silent hand in greeting.

"You waited for me," she said as she approached him, feeling dumb for stating the obvious but unable to resist making the statement.

"I figured, since I'm the one who brought you here, you'd need me to take you back as well," John said, smiling as he got up. "I wasn't going to just abandon you here, even if your partner was coming. I wanted to make sure you had a way to get home."

"Thank you," Zoe said, floored by the generosity with his time. Not to mention the fact that it was cold out, and he had sat outside to wait for her. He hadn't needed to do any of that. She hadn't asked him to. In fact, she now realized with a faint embarrassment, she had probably been fairly rude to walk away from him without saying goodbye.

"So, where do you want to go?" John asked, his hands in his pockets as he rocked gently on the balls of his feet. "Consider me your taxi driver. Home? Back to the bar? Somewhere else?"

Zoe thought about it. She didn't want to go home. She could barely face the thought. Going back to the bar was a bad idea, and a waste of time. Getting drunk wasn't going to help her solve this case. Any more alcohol and she would probably be crying in John's lap about how badly she had messed up. A mental image which did not at all fit with the way she wanted others to see her.

"I need to go see my friend," she decided. "The one I told you about, who got arrested because of me. She is at the local precinct. Will you take me there?"

"Of course." John smiled warmly, making a short bow and gesturing in the direction of the car. "The lady's wish is my command. Let's go."

Zoe couldn't quite tell whether he was mocking her or being nice, but since he was taking her where she needed to go, she decided that it didn't matter.

Zoe's travel sickness was worse than ever as they drove the quiet and near-deserted roads, even though the ride was slower and smoother than the previous journey. The alcohol in her bloodstream was already working its way out of her system, wearing off. Now it was the nausea that came after a drink, as well as the existing reaction to the motion of the car. Just exactly what she needed on a night when everything else seemed to be going so badly wrong around her.

"You didn't get what you wanted in there, did you?" John asked, not taking his eyes off the road. Zoe appreciated that. It made him seem a more responsible driver.

"No." Zoe paused, wondering. "How could you tell?"

"You were so fired up on the way here, thinking you'd figured it all out. Now, not so much. I expected you'd be happy if things had worked out the way you thought."

Zoe took this in, watching the road ahead just as he was. It was a strange sensation, both of them observing this sight together, talking without turning to one another. More comfortable than other conversations, where Zoe had to try and give some kind of facial expression to avoid appearing like a robot, had to try and decipher the meaningless expressions and gestures she saw from others.

"I was wrong," she admitted, at last. "I do not know how. It still seems like it would all fit perfectly. But the answer was not there."

"I guess life's a little like that," John said, pausing to concentrate as he turned right onto a new road. "Even when we want things to fit perfectly, they have a way of breaking the pattern."

He was right. Zoe lived her life through patterns, saw them everywhere, understood them intimately. But when it came to real life—human behavior, interactions, feelings—the patterns were often defied.

"It would be a lot neater if it was not this way."

John gave a short laugh. "It sure would. Easier, too."

At least they could agree on that. Zoe was still turning this over in her mind when the car stopped, pulling her out of her thoughts to the extent that she looked around in confusion.

"We're here," John explained, turning in his seat now to face her. "Anything else I can do for you, before I go?"

Zoe disengaged her seatbelt, taking a deep breath of air. Still air. A blessing. "You have done more than enough," she said. She felt there should be something in it for him—some kind of reward. Dr. Monk had been telling her to make an effort. Perhaps now was the most appropriate time to put that into practice. "Thank you for everything tonight. We should meet again, sometime when I am not in the middle of a case."

John beamed, not bothering to hide his delight. Zoe appreciated that. Too many men still acted like children. Hiding their emotions and expecting her to guess. She was never going to be able to guess. "I'll take you up on that," he said. "Call me when you're done with this one. We can go for another meal, maybe."

"I will. I would like that." Zoe hesitated, unsure if she had done a proper job of ticking off all the niceties that were expected of her. "Well, then I will see you soon."

"Goodnight, Zoe," John said, giving her a look that she felt perhaps indicated the conversation was over and she was free to depart.

Whether it actually did or not, she had no way of knowing, but it was as good a guess as any.

Zoe had been worried for a brief moment that she might be waking Dr. Applewhite up, but being held by the FBI for the first time in your life was not a soothing experience. She had been sitting awake, staring at the walls, with nothing else to do to pass the time.

"I am sorry for all of this," Zoe said quietly, sitting opposite her mentor with a steaming cup of coffee in front of both of them. The staff on duty had insisted that if she wanted to talk to someone being held overnight, it had to be in a proper interrogation room. It had to be recorded.

It wasn't the way she would have preferred to do things, but it would have to do.

"The wheels of justice have to keep on turning." Dr. Applewhite smiled, tucking her hair behind her ear. She didn't sound particularly happy, even if her lips were curved up into the right shape.

"Is that a quotation?"

"At this stage, I don't even know." Dr. Applewhite sipped at her coffee. "I'm tired, Zoe. It's been a long day."

The guilt hit her even harder. What more could she do? It wasn't as if Zoe had been sitting around at home, or had resolved just to leave Dr. Applewhite in a cell all night. She had been out there, trying to find a solution for this thing. It just hadn't happened.

"I am sorry," Zoe murmured again, wondering if at this point it even made any difference. She continued louder, wanting to take action now more than ever. "I have been working on a theory. I thought you might be able to help me figure out who the culprit could be."

"Anything to get me out of here quicker." Dr. Applewhite sighed. "Let's hear it, then."

Zoe nodded. "I think the killer has recently suffered some kind of neurological change. One side effect of this would be something like aphasia, dyslexia, dyscalculia. Something that prevents him from being able to write things out properly. That is why the equations do not make sense, and also why the violence has started happening now. I am willing to bet that before this traumatic event, whatever it was, the killer has no history of violent behavior."

"But?"

"But we went to the hospital where Dr. North worked, and there was nothing in the records. We cannot find anyone who fits the criteria of this kind of recent development alongside the appropriate height, weight, and age."

"Hmm." Dr. Applewhite took another sip of her coffee. "Well, the theory works. It doesn't sound like it should be wrong."

"That is why I thought you might be of some help. I need you to think back, wrack your brains. Is there anyone, either in the academic world or in mathematical circles? Anyone who was rumored to be a bit strange, or stories that sound a bit off? Glaring mistakes, problems with speech, anything like that?"

Dr. Applewhite sat back in her chair, her eyes roving across pictures that Zoe could not see as she thought. "Mistakes, yes. But those are just part of mathematics. That's what happens when you try to work on something difficult, something theoretical. My own formula was flawed, after all."

"Not something like that—not a missed calculation or a failure to carry the one. More like things being written down in the wrong way. Numbers reversed, or put out of order, for example. The way that the equations on the bodies were unbalanced."

"I work too much to stay up to date with all of the national journals, to read something as embarrassing as that," Dr. Applewhite protested. "I suppose it would have made a scandal, but I haven't heard about anyone messing up that badly."

"It does not need to have been published. It could have been coursework—something a professor at the college noticed and mentioned to you. Someone brilliant that suddenly made mistakes. It has to be a big fall from grace for him to be this angry. If I suddenly lost the ability to draw, given my already limited art skills, I do not think that I would be upset."

"That's very insightful. You've been working on your empathetic understanding of others, haven't you?"

Zoe couldn't say that she had, but maybe just being around someone like Shelley was enough to help her understand more about human nature, in herself and others. "That is not the point. Think back. Stories, rumors. Hints. Anything you heard in passing. It does not even have to be concrete."

"Look, I just can't think of anyone," Dr. Applewhite said. "Maybe it would be better to ask the professors. Or another neurologist."

"The change might not have been completely obvious," Zoe pressed. She couldn't give up. Not when they were this close to getting somewhere. If she wasn't right about this, then Dr. Applewhite could go all the way to trial. "The brain—it does not always work in the ways that we expect. Maybe he could have hidden his communication problems by talking less, going underground or something. But someone would have noticed. His personality would be different, he would be quieter. Not as able to perform at the level he was at previously. A star student, suddenly not on the scene anymore."

"The only students that normally get referred to me by others are the ones who show signs of synesthesia. Not very many, as you might appreciate. Even when we talk about these things, it's not normally by name."

"I don't even need a name," Zoe pleaded. How could Dr. Applewhite not see that she needed her to try harder, to dig deeper? This could mean the difference between going home in the morning and staying here to await trial, if the killer didn't strike again. "Just a hint. Someone else we can talk to who might know something. Anything at all."

Dr. Applewhite was frowning, looking off into the distance. "What was that you said about going quieter?"

"A—a star student," Zoe said, desperately trying to remember her exact words. "His personality would change and he would go quiet. No longer performing at the same level."

Dr. Applewhite paused, rubbing her lips with the side of her index finger as she thought. "I ... I think there might have been something like that," she said.

"Who? When?" Zoe practically felt like she was about to leap across the table and rip the words out of Dr. Applewhite's head herself, if that would make them come out quicker.

"I don't know why I didn't think of it before. It was—yes—I'm sure of it—it was Ralph Henderson."

"The English professor who died?"

"There was a student of his, someone who showed a lot of promise. Ralph told me about how it was such a shame. He had been in an accident or something—a car crash or something like that. Ralph was thinking of recommending him for some advanced training, getting him to work on more theoretical stuff, but after the accident he retreated. He didn't say anything about the effects on his work—given that he was teaching English, not math—or about him being unable to communicate. Just that he wasn't so active on campus, retreated into himself, started missing lectures."

"Do you know his name?" This was it. The million-dollar question. If they could just find him ...

Dr. Applewhite screwed up her face. "Oh, god, this was a while ago ... and I wasn't even really listening at the time. Let me try to think. I didn't get any of the details—god, what did he keep calling him?"

Zoe kept quiet, biting her tongue. Dr. Applewhite needed space to think. Zoe counted seconds, trying not to explode. If she could just keep quiet for thirty—no, maybe sixty seconds—just long enough for Dr. Applewhite to get there ...

"It was . . . it was something unusual," Dr. Applewhite said. She rubbed her temples, trying so hard to get there. "Something kind of exotic. God, why can't I remember?"

"Something unusual," Zoe repeated. "And the student, he was at Georgetown, right? He took classes with Ralph Henderson, at least for a while."

"Yes, he must have. Otherwise I don't know why Ralph would have been thinking about putting him forward."

It wasn't a whole lot, but it was something. It was a starting point. From the whole of the state down to one college, and from the whole student population of the college down to those who took certain classes. It might not get them a list of one, but it would definitely get them closer—and even if they ended up with a list of fifty, they could work through it. They could ask questions, check alibis, request medical records.

"I will call you if we get anything," Zoe said, getting up. "Try to get some rest. By the morning, we might be putting the real killer in your place."

She left the room and a weary Dr. Applewhite behind, indicating that she was done to the guards on duty as she dug out her phone to call Shelley.

"I have something real," Zoe said, as soon as the line connected. "He is a student. Dr. Applewhite remembered Ralph Henderson talking about him. We can narrow it down."

There was a groan on Shelley's side. "Z, I literally just got back into bed."

"This cannot wait until the morning," Zoe protested.

"I know." A sigh. "I just wish you had called before I took my makeup off and got changed—again. I'll be at HQ in fifteen."

Zoe pocketed her phone and strode along with new purpose, sure now that they were only hours away from having the killer in cuffs.

Chapter Twenty Four

Zoe stood behind the FBI tech, watching him load up a database. The raw data from the Georgetown student list was vast, but it was the starting point. They had to go from there.

Next to her, Shelley had her arms folded across her chest, and she was leaning forward to get the screen in clearer focus. She had not bothered to neatly redo her chignon this time, opting for a simple ponytail. It made her look more youthful.

"All right, we're loaded up," the tech said, flexing his fingers over the keyboard. "Where are we looking?"

"First, they should be a student who took a class with Professor Ralph Henderson in the last semester," Shelley said.

"Two semesters, just to be sure," Zoe interjected. "Also include any extracurricular activities he led, if there are any."

The tech ran his fingers over the keyboard and made a few clicks, and the names on the screen flashed a few times before reloading in a new order.

"We have one hundred and fifty results. Anything else to refine it by?"

"Yes—males only."

Another couple of clicks and the list flashed, reloaded. A much smaller selection. "Down to ninety."

"Now cross-reference with students that have also taken any kind of class with the mathematics department," Zoe said.

"Would he have been majoring in math?" Shelley asked.

"Hard to say." Zoe chewed her bottom lip. "It is possible, but then again perhaps he had not yet chosen a major at all before the accident. We should stick to any kind of math class."

Flash; reload. They didn't need the tech to announce the results this time. They all fit on a single view—fifty-three students.

"Move over so we can read them," Zoe said, peering over his head. The font size was small, too small for easy viewing.

The tech leaned back to look at her face, to see if she was being serious. When he saw that she was, he sighed, and scooted his chair to one side.

Zoe and Shelley stepped forward in unison, each leaning one hand on the desk so that they could make out the names more easily. Adam, Alex, Alexander, Alexei...Even with the knowledge they were looking for something "exotic," there were still too many options. It was a tough variable to define—what would Dr. Applewhite even define as exotic? Did Alexei fit the bill or was it too common? What about Govinder, lower on the list? Could it be him?

"We need to narrow it down more," Shelley said, as if reading Zoe's mind. "This is going to take too long."

"There's one thing we can do. We're thinking that this student would have to have been brilliant—someone who would have been trusted by Wardenford to look at his equations. That means he has to have been getting good grades."

"Where do I click?" Shelley asked, looking to the tech for instructions. He leaned over to point out the sorting areas on the screen, helping her to select anyone who was getting either perfect scores or almost perfect on tests and papers, the ones in the class with the best grades.

There were still twenty-two students on the list. It was a good school, after all.

Shelley blew out a sigh, rubbing her eyes. "Marco, can you print this out for us? Just the ones we noted, please."

Marco rolled his chair back across as they stepped out of the way, getting to work.

"Should we start going to their houses?" Zoe suggested. It was the middle of the night, but that didn't mean they had to stand on ceremony. They were looking for a serial killer in the middle of a spree, after all.

"We could," Shelley said, then rubbed her eyes again. "It's a shame. This is going to take us all night."

Zoe looked over the list. Something was nagging at her memory, snagging her eye as she ran down the names.

The letters—the capital letters. Could that be it?

"The equations—there was something odd about them," she said, opening her notebook to the page where she had copied them out. "Look here—see? The 'M' is a capital. But here—on Dr. Applewhite's version of the equation, before it was jumbled by the killer: the 'm' is lowercase. It indicates magnetic quantum value. The lowercase from is correct."

"Assigning significance to a letter." Shelley nodded. "It's very likely to be a letter that he writes as a capital often. One of his initials. Zoe, that's brilliant!"

"Two Matthews and one Matthias," Zoe read, checking the list.

"That's all of them. No, wait—the surnames. There's a Matthew there as well."

"Only Matthias is what I would call exotic," Zoe noted. "And—look at this. He has not been attending class for a while. His grades sharply dropped, then disappeared altogether."

"This must be our guy!" Shelley was enthusiastic, her eyes gleaming.

Zoe nodded. "But what about his medical records? He didn't show up on Dr. North's list. Can we be sure he has a connection to him?"

Shelley was tapping a pen against her lower lip, her eyes glazed with that particular look that accompanies deep thought. "You know," she said, slowly, as if she was still figuring it out while she said it. "I've been thinking about something the administrator at the hospital said. He told us he could only check one site, as if he was expecting us to look at records for other hospitals as well. Specialist doctors don't always just have one hospital where they work."

"What?"

"Well, Dr. North was a specialist, right? A neurosurgeon? Sometimes they will be on staff at a couple of different places in the same area, so that the skills are on hand wherever they're needed."

"Call the hospital and find out where else he worked," Zoe said, her eyes widening as she grasped what Shelley was saying. "I will try to find a judge who might let us have a warrant so they will release the information."

As it turned out, she need not have bothered. Zoe had just finished checking schedules and figuring out that Judge Lopez was going to be in court in the morning, but didn't have a trial until a little later on, when Shelley burst back into their little investigation room from the corridor where she had been making her call.

"They're faxing us through the patient records," Shelley said. Despite the late hour and her lack of sleep, she was grinning. "I gave them Matthias Kranz and they were able to pick up his records at a hospital on the north side of the city. I told the administrator there it was a matter of life or death, told him this was Dr. North's killer, and he was happy to bend the rules. Matthias saw last Dr. North two months ago. Even better—he was scheduled for follow-up appointments that he never attended. It sounds like he could have gone rogue. We'll know more when they send his full records through."

Zoe could hardly wait for the antiquated machine to stop printing. She counted how many lines had already come through and calculated the per-page printing speed, feeling despair each time it started on a new page and utter relief when it finally spat out half a page at the end.

She almost tore them in her haste to snatch them up and start leafing through them, searching for something that would make sense.

"Anything?" Shelley asked, almost crowding into her and backing off when Zoe made an impatient gesture.

"Give me a chance to read it. Hold on ..." Zoe skimmed the words, flipping pages to his most recent records. "Here. TBI—traumatic brain injury from a car accident sustained two months and twenty-four days ago. Matthias was a passenger and his head hit the dashboard during the crash, after the car's airbags failed to deflate."

"Probably an old model. Students aren't known for being able to afford particularly road-worthy vehicles," Shelley commented.

"He suffered cuts and bruises, but nothing else until he started complaining of headaches and confusion. He was put through a number of tests—CT scan, blood tests, X-ray, MRI, PET ... then visual, audio, everything Dr. North could think of. Finally he was diagnosed one month and thirty days ago. Aphasia and dyslexia as an ongoing result of the TBI, with no suggestions for treatment other than managing the symptoms."

"It's permanent?"

"The doctor recommended that Matthias attend counselling sessions as well as a class for improved cognitive development, but it says here that he never attended. He did not cancel, just did not show up."

"This is definitely him, isn't it?" Shelley grinned.

"It is just what I was looking for," Zoe confirmed, flipping back to the first page of the records. "We have his address and contact number here. It looks like he lives just off campus."

"Then let's hope he's there," Shelley said, grabbing her jacket from the back of a chair. "We need to bring him in, now."

They drove out of the J. Edgar Hoover Building parking lot into the startling blue of an extremely early morning, the sun newly risen. It was still hidden behind the tall architecture around them, and Zoe and Shelley were in shadow as they picked up speed in the direction of the Georgetown campus.

It didn't matter, Zoe thought. They were going to be out in the light soon.

Chapter Twenty Five

James Wardenford cursed and rubbed his eyes, wishing he had been able to get back to sleep. After spending that time with the FBI and going through the withdrawal process from his precious alcohol, he had figured, what the hell? Why not try and go through with it this time?

It wouldn't be the first time he had tried to quit, and he was quietly not very confident in himself that it would be the last. Mornings like this were to blame. He had come to rely on alcohol to get him to sleep, and without it he was half-insomniac. Staying up all night feverish and itchy, finally nodding off only to wake up before dawn. His body felt like it was eating itself. Still, that was supposed to stop soon, right?

Wardenford dressed slowly, cursing again at the aching in his limbs. Life wasn't supposed to be this hard. He wasn't an old man yet. He'd played a tough hand for his body to take, though, and it was letting its complaints be known now that he didn't have a good whiskey to smooth the pain away.

He was dressed and sitting at his kitchen table with a mug of coffee, trying to pretend to himself that it was Irish, when someone rang his buzzer.

"Hello?" he said, frowning. It wouldn't be those FBI girls again, would it? He'd enjoyed going over a puzzle with the smart one, and the other one wasn't unpleasant to look at, but he'd had enough interrogations to last him a lifetime. Besides, that was where all this discomfort had started, with the sweating and the shakes.

"Professor?"

Wardenford's mind was blank for a moment, appreciating that the sentiment must indicate a student but unsure about the voice. "It's just Mr. Wardenford now," he settled for.

"Sorry, right. It's Matthias Kranz. I wanted to catch up. If it's too early, I can go away."

Matthias Kranz! Now, there was a student. One of the brightest of the bright. Although, hadn't Wardenford heard through the grapevine that he never did end up taking a place on that program? Maybe he could ask him about it now.

Besides, Matthias had always been a polite and respectful boy. It would be nice to see someone who treated him the way he had been used to, back when he still had the support of the community.

"It's fine—I'm an early riser at the moment. Please come up."

After pushing the buzzer to unlock the door several stories below, Wardenford glanced around at the apartment and down at himself. His clothes were fine, if a little informal—the boy was used to seeing him in a suit jacket, not a sweater—but the décor could do with some hasty rearranging. He closed the door to his bedroom to shut out the mess, and did a rapid sweep of the open-plan kitchen, diner, and living area, throwing away empty bottles and takeout cartons. He even threw away a dirty plate in his haste, having far too little time to get it washed up and put away.

The knock on the door came before he was quite done, but it would have to do. An apartment that was too clean, too tidy—well, that smacked of a tidy-up, didn't it? Better for there to be a few things out of place here and there, to give a lived-in impression. Wardenford caught his breath for a brief moment, before heading over and opening the door.

"Matthias," he said warming, greeting his former student with a handshake. "How have you been? Come in, come in."

"I'm well," Matthias said, in a manner that seemed almost reticent. "You?"

Wardenford thought his lack of verboseness might be down to the awkward feeling of meeting someone one is used to seeing in a position of authority, but was now on level footing. Certainly, he had once been extremely talkative, and they had enjoyed many bright and spirited debates after his classes. In favor of improving his impression, Wardenford decided on the spot to ad lib a little. "Oh, just great, yes. I've been keeping myself busy with some consultation work."

Well, the FBI had asked him for his opinion, hadn't they?

Matthias sat down silently on the sofa when Wardenford gestured for him to do so, offering a slim smile. These bright kids—it was always hard to tell with them, wasn't it? They hadn't spent a great deal of time developing social skills, usually, and so while they were excellent at navigating classes and partnering up for assignments, talking out of class was another thing.

"Would you like a coffee?" Wardenford asked, checking the temperature of the glass and pouring himself a top-up. "It's fresh-made."

"Yes, please," Matthias said, and Wardenford was buoyed by this.

With the two cups steaming on the coffee table and both of the men seated comfortably, Wardenford found that he was going to have to carry the conversation. Matthias had not said anything more. Rather than asking him outright why he had come—a question to which he might not like the answer, particularly if it turned out to deflate his ego—Wardenford decided to take this opportunity to extract any and all gossip he could about his former faculty.

"So, what's new at Georgetown?"

"People are mostly talking about the bodies." There was a measured, deliberate way to the way that Matthias spoke now. Like he was choosing each word carefully, and with great effort. What had happened to him . . . ?

"Of course, of course." Wardenford nodded. "I'm sure there's a lot of upset about it. Professor Henderson was a much-loved member of the staff."

"Yes." Matthias sipped at his coffee, his face largely blank.

"You had lectures with him as well, didn't you? I seem to recall you mentioning that you were taking some English classes alongside your physics and mathematics."

Matthias nodded. "I stopped."

"Oh, well, that's a shame." Wardenford paused. "Not for you, necessarily. After all, you can take whichever classes seem best fitted to your needs. I simply mean, I would like to know how things are now. I presume there will be a TA or one of the other members of staff filling in. Have you heard if they have engaged a new lecturer for his position yet?"

Matthias shook his head. "I'm just glad the real killer has been caught."

One thing about that struck Wardenford as odd, and then as he thought about it more, two things. The "real" killer? Did Matthias know that he had been arrested and spoken to?

Did everyone know it?

The other point was that Wardenford had thought he was the only one to know about the latest development. Had the police somehow made it public overnight? He had checked both local and national news this morning, and seen no updates about an arrest in the case.

"Caught?" he replied, treading cautiously. "Did they say who it was?"

Matthias made a face. "Pear. Uh, white. Pear white. No, something…"

"Dr. Applewhite," Wardenford corrected quietly. So. They really had arrested her. Well. When he had presented what he could see himself, the equations pointing the way, he did not know if he really believed it could be true. But if they had taken her in—"How did you hear about that? I haven't seen anything in the news."

Matthias shrugged. He was depending on gestures today, Wardenford noticed. Fewer words and more gestures. As if he was unwilling to spare any more words to get his point across. "Campus rumors," he said.

Ah, yes. The old rumor mill. Wardenford had been quite fond of it once, before he became the headline story for a while. Since then, of course, he had barely heard a thing. Even if someone had been willing to tell him, he wouldn't have remembered any of it, not with the amount he had been drinking.

Still, it sent a shiver down his spine. News traveled fast around here, and if someone had managed to see Dr. Applewhite being arrested and spread it around the campus already, it seemed quite likely that they had done the same for him. So, another dent to his already battered reputation.

Mind you, at least he had been released. Maybe that would help matters.

The sound of a car horn blaring outside startled Wardenford, and he rose to look out the window. "Goodness me," he muttered, shaking his head. "They shouldn't be making that kind of racket this early in the morning. Some people are still asleep. What time is it now, anyway?"

"It's nine-sixteen."

Nine-sixteen…? That didn't sound right, surely? Had so many hours flown by while Wardenford was staring into the bottom of a coffee cup? No, and the city was still quiet, people only just getting onto their commutes, school buses just starting to go past for the first time. Wardenford glanced at his watch, scratched and battered from many a drinking session that ended badly, and saw that he was right.

It was six-nineteen.

He opened his mouth to laugh and tell Matthias that he had got it the wrong way around, but then stopped himself. Hang on a second, here, James, he told himself. Now, just hang on and think about this.

The equations were all jumbled up, all out of order. The numbers, the letters, in the wrong places.

And Matthias was speaking so carefully, with so much control, using as few words as he possibly could.

Not that there was any need to read too far into that, was there? Perhaps he was overtired. Yes, that was probably all. To read any more into it would be absurd.

"Well," Wardenford said briskly, turning back from the window and resuming his spot on the sofa. "Some people just don't have any sense of what's right, do they? I imagine there was barely any reason for them to hit the horn at all. You know what these road-rage inner-city drivers are like."

Matthias laughed politely, nodding his head.

And Wardenford remembered something—something he had not thought of for a long time. The equation that Dr. Applewhite had shared with him. The fact that he had then shared it with Matthias, hoping that the lad would be able to use his talents to find the correction.

He'd been working on it, hadn't he? Back then. Before the scandal hit.

Matthias had seen the equation, and there was something wrong with him now. The numbers. He had mixed up the numbers when he read the time.

Just like the numbers had been mixed up in the equations.

And, oh god, there it was: Matthias had been a student of Henderson's. He'd known Cole. God, there it all was.

It was him.

This benign-looking, innocuous student. This college dropout who had once had everything at his feet thanks to his supreme intelligence. This boy who Wardenford had spoken with and come to know, and hoped to lead to greatness.

He was a murderer.

Wardenford made sure to smile at him, willing himself to carry it right through to his eyes. Matthias had never been stupid, and he wasn't now. If there was any way that he suspected that Wardenford knew who he really was—and, he realized with an extra thrill of fear—why he was really there, it would be over.

Because Matthias Kranz wasn't there for a cup of coffee and a nice chat about old times.

He was there to murder James Wardenford.

Chapter Twenty Six

Zoe hit the brake hard and quickly shifted into reverse. "Damn it! This one?"

"Yeah, down there," Shelley said, doing her best to juggle her attention between the GPS and the phone in her hand. "No, not you, Fred. Right. And there's no connection?"

Zoe didn't like the way Shelley's conversation sounded like it was going. They were flying blind at the moment, heading for Matthias Kranz's student housing because it was the only logical lead that they had as to his location. A trace on his cell would make it a lot easier to track him down, but Shelley didn't seem to be getting anywhere with setting that up.

"Okay. Keep an eye on it, please, Fred. Just let me know as soon as it pops up again. This is an active pursuit, okay? Thanks. You're a star. Okay, talk later."

Shelley ended the call, shifting in the passenger seat and looking around. "It should be one of these ones coming up, right? Fred says he can't get a trace on the kid's cell. We'll just have to hope that he's home."

"Why do I feel like I already know he is not?" Zoe growled, slowing down as she peered through the side windows at numbers posted outside of houses.

"Because you're an optimistic, happy-go-lucky kind of gal," Shelley joked, without so much as cracking a smile. "Here. It's this one."

Shelley was out of the car and halfway across the sidewalk by the time Zoe had managed to get it into park, and she was a few steps behind still by the time Shelley was banging on the front door.

"I will go around the back," she said, spotting a dilapidated wooden door in the poorly maintained fence between the house and the one next to it. Sure enough, the door flew open without much effort on her part, the wood too dry and old to fit snugly into the frame anymore. It wasn't locked.

At the back of the house, a yard grown almost knee-high with weeds and grasses took up only fifteen feet by ten—enough for it to attract a higher price tag, but apparently not enough for the student residents to want to take care of it.

Zoe assessed the back of the house: two sets of windows on the ground floor, three sets of windows above, almost the same as the front. The difference was that the middle window was small and slotted—a bathroom window, not big enough for anyone to climb out of. Still, Zoe kept her eye on the others for a sign of movement.

It was the back door that opened instead, and her instinct to spring toward it and prevent anyone from leaving was met with owlish concern from a young man in spectacles. He was five foot four—short for a male, and certainly too short to be their killer.

"Your partner told me to let you in," he said, leaning back away from her as if concerned that she would tackle him. "She headed upstairs to check the rooms, but I told her there's no point. Matthias isn't here. He went out early this morning."

"How early?" Zoe asked, stepping inside. From here, she could see both the front and back exits. A good enough place to wait for Shelley to finish her checks, in case someone decided to make a break for it.

"I don't know, man. Before I woke up. His shoes are gone, that's how I know."

"Do you have any idea where he went?"

"No." The student seemed taken aback, confused even, by her questioning. "What's this about?"

"This is about an FBI investigation, which you are obstructing if you do not answer all of our questions truthfully," Zoe snapped. Perhaps Shelley wouldn't have approved, but there was no time for the light touch here. Lives were at stake. "Think very carefully. Do you have any idea—even the smallest clue—about where Matthias is right now?"

The kid was still half-asleep, clearly, but that seemed to snap him awake. "Uh, okay, okay, just let me think! Uh . . . well, last night he said something."

"What did he say?" Zoe asked, impatient and angry that she even had to ask the question to drag the information out of him.

"He talked about this guy who used to be his professor. He got, like, fired or something. Or quit, I don't know. Anyway, Matthias was saying how he wanted to go check the guy was good or whatever. I don't know. I thought it sounded kind of dumb, but Matthias actually likes his professors, you know? Like they're people. Not like they're professors or whatever."

Zoe could barely contain her exasperation. As if professors were not people. This young man needed some sense put into him, but there was hardly any time to address that now. "Which professor? What was his name?"

"Oh, uh... I don't think he gave me a name," the student stuttered.

Shelley clattered down the stairs, the heels of her shoes striking each of the steps with a staccato cacophony. "Upper floor is clear," she said.

"Did you check down here?"

"No. Watch the doors." Shelley disappeared from view momentarily, first on one side of the hall and then on the other, as she checked the downstairs rooms. Then she was out again, shaking her head.

"This one says Matthias went to visit an old professor."

"Mathematics?"

"I don't know!" The student raised his hands, looking back and forth between both of them. "I swear, I have no idea. I don't even *like* Matthias. This was just a cheap option so we could split the rent. We got matched up by this service at the college. Seriously, I don't know where he spends his time."

Shelley snapped her fingers, apparently struck by sudden inspiration. "Was it James Wardenford?"

"Oh, yeah," the student replied, shrugging his shoulders. "Now that you said it, I remember. Yeah. Professor Wardenford."

"You have been almost useless," Zoe informed him, before nodding to Shelley and leading the way back out of the building.

"I'm calling him now," Shelley said, hitting buttons on her cell and lifting it to her ear. "We'd better get over to his apartment. If Matthias is there right now, he's in danger."

"And probably stinking drunk," Zoe remarked, getting back behind the wheel of the car.

Shelley slid into the passenger seat, then swore and took the cell from her ear. "No answer. I'll try him again."

Zoe paused only to search for the address in her GPS—easy enough to find, since she knew how many places she had been since then and could simply choose the right option in the history—before hitting the accelerator and pulling out. "How did you think of Wardenford?"

Shelley was playing with her pendant with the hand that wasn't holding her cell. "He was dismissed before Matthias had his accident. If he's been out of the loop, he might be the only person from Georgetown who Matthias had contact with that doesn't know about it. Either that, or Matthias has already been to him for help before and Wardenford figured out what was wrong, and now Matthias wants revenge. I don't know. Wardenford didn't mention Matthias when we knew the equations were all tangled up. I'm guessing he would still be in the dark."

"Why would he go there, if not to kill him?" Zoe frowned, hitting the gas to avoid colliding with a slow-moving car as she made a sharp turn.

"If he isn't aware that Matthias has been having any difficulties, then he could represent the last person from Matthias's old life who will act as though nothing has happened. Treat him as though he's still as capable as he was. That could be huge for him."

Zoe thought about it. She had something that was entirely the opposite: the relief of being around the very few people who did know her diagnosis, and no longer having to pretend that she was like everyone else. But if everyone knew, except from a select few? She could see how there might be comfort in that, too. If her cover was blown and people started treating her even more like an alien, then she would want to go back to the one person who still thought she was just rude and aloof.

"But Wardenford knows about the equations now," Zoe realized. "If he connects the dots in any way—if Matthias somehow shows his hand—"

Shelley finished her thought. "Matthias will kill him."

Zoe pushed her foot down further on the accelerator. This was a matter of timing only. Either they got there before Wardenford was murdered, or after.

She hoped to god that it would be before.

Chapter Twenty Seven

Matthias shook his head. He was getting the hang of this now. The focus. He was able to get the words out. "I'm just glad the real killer has been caught." There! See! A whole th—a th—a sentence. A whole sentence.

He was too busy being proud of himself to watch Waterfo—*Wardenford*. But when he spoke he sounded nervous, like his head snakes were all swimming, like something churned within him.

"Caught? Did they say who it was?"

Matthias twisted his face up with the concentration. Say it. Say. The words. Come on. "Pear. Uh, white. Pear white. No, something..." He knew he was so far off. So far off. He was about to get caught. Wardenford would know. He would know about Matthias's snakes and how they all slithered in the wrong direction now.

"Dr. Applewhite," Wardenford corrected quietly. "How did you hear about that? I haven't seen anything in the news."

Mistake, mistake! Didn't check the news, didn't read the—scrolls. Should have checked. Oh, Matthias, you got yourself caught. Those snakes were getting away.

Matthias shrugged to get the message down to as few words as he could. He couldn't risk it, not now, with the—picnic in him. Not picnic. *Focus*. Explain it. "Campus rumors," he said.

There was silence. Maybe Matthias said too much. Maybe the picnic—the *panic* was justified. Oh, but how awful it would be if he knew! If he saw the snakes!

A loud noise outside, and Wardenford rose to look out the window. "Goodness me," he muttered, shaking his head. "They shouldn't be making that kind of racket this early in the morning. Some people are still asleep. What time is it now, anyway?"

Matthias looked at his watch. Read it confidently without thinking. "It's nine-sixteen."

There was a long silence.

Matthias saw Wardenford look back at his watch and checked his own again. Focused. Squinted his eyes one way, then another. Wardenford was still looking outside. The time was wrong. The time he read out was wrong.

"Well," Wardenford said, turning back from the glass and sitting on the—bench. "Some people just don't have any sense of what's right, do they? I imagine there was barely any reason for them to hit the horn at all. You know what these road-rage inner-city drivers are like."

Wardenford gave his happy smile. Matthias looked at him and smiled back, and behind it all the snakes were foaming. He knew. Wardenford knew.

What a stupid mistake.

But maybe all was not—gone. After all, his mentor could guess about the snakes. The mind snakes. That didn't mean he knew about the *blood* snakes.

"I try not to drive," Matthias said. He had to be careful because he could not find his way to the word for the thing that people drove, the—refuge, and he had to control his expression as well. Wardenford might just think it was a one-off mistake. Not snakes but silliness. Maybe Matthias could pretend it was a—funny.

It wasn't true, anyway. He'd been driving a lot, lately. But at least if he said he didn't, he could distance himself from the suspicion. A killer didn't get on the sub-sub—coach.

Wardenford hadn't said anything for a minute. He was looking at his coffee. Matthias wondered if he was figuring it out.

"I haven't driven at all, since . . ." Wardenford began, then stopped. "Well. All that unpleasantness. Best left in the past. Anyway, how are your studies going?"

Matthias picked up his coffee and sipped. Best left in the past too. But a direct question needed an answer. "Dropped out," he said. Immediately he was unhappy smiles, raging at himself, the snakes all hissing and biting their own tails. Such an answer would mean—following. He would have to talk more. He looked into the black coffee and hoped it would end there, knowing it wouldn't.

Wardenford set his coffee down on the table, ringing, ringing, ringing. "You dropped out? Matthias, what happened? You were doing so well when I left. One of my best students. Are you planning to study somewhere else?"

Matthias shook his snakes slowly.

"Good god. It must have been bad, whatever it was. Is it money? You can't afford the tuition anymore? Please tell me it's something like that, something we can fix. There are grants I can help you to apply for."

Matthias shook his snakes again, slow, slow, slow.

Wardenford swallowed. His—pear bobbed up and down in his throat. He must have been nervous, Matthias realized. He was trying not to show it.

"Just let me know if there's something I can do to help," Wardenford said at last. "If you don't want to talk about it just now, I understand."

Matthias looked down into his coffee. Drank a bit. Wardenford knew about the snakes.

Not just the head snakes.

The blood snakes.

"Actually, you know, I do have to get somewhere," Wardenford said, his voice suddenly pepping up. "I hadn't realized the time. But what with it being so far on, I should really get ready. It's been wonderful to see you, Matthias. Do come visit again. And consider my offer for help, yes?"

He stood up, a gesture that was clearly designed to show Matthias it was time to leave.

Could he leave?

Matthias didn't want to do it but the head snakes, they needed it. They couldn't stop with the blood and the headbox couldn't contain them—not his headbox, not Wardenford's headbox. They had to come out. There was an ache in Matthias's chest, in his—his chestbox—his ven—ca—what was it, the thing in the chestbox—the thing... oh, it ached with the thought of ending him. The snakes were wrapping around it and squeezing their tails tight, but what could he do?

He couldn't spare him. If it wasn't for all of the others—but the snakes were on his hands, written in letters so big Wardenford could read them now, and he knew. He would tell. Even if Matthias begged him not to, he would tell. He had to be stopped.

It was a mistake, coming here. He had wanted comfort, the words of an old mentor. Now Wardenford would pay in blood snakes, would pay for them like all the others. It was his fault. He shouldn't have come. But there was no going back. Matthias had to do it. He had to do it now.

The—buzzing box on the table rang, a fun happy tune ringing out across the space, lighting up the display. In a flash, Matthias had to think: think, think. If he answered, Wardenford could tell them. Could bring the flashing lights and men with guns and put him away forever. That couldn't happen.

That couldn't be.

He saw an empty wine bottle sitting beside the sofa, down right by the edge, where Wardenford missed it when he was cleaning. He saw it clearly. Everything was aligned.

Matthias took the bottle and lunged forward and smashed the full force of it over Wardenford's headbox, and the man fell to the floor with a startled groan, and it was done.

The buzzingbox rang again on the table, into the silence now of the room. Matthias stood above him, catching his breath, feeling the snakes writhe around in his own headbox in anticipation of the blood to come.

Chapter Twenty Eight

Zoe remembered the way from their last visit. She raced up the stairs, taking them two at a time, then counted doors the flashed by until she was at the right one. Behind it she could hear nothing, as she paused in the corridor and waited for that long second.

Shelley caught up, panting, as Zoe pressed the call button on her cell again. They both heard the ringtone faintly on the other side, going unanswered. They exchanged a look.

The situation was precarious. If the killer was inside, they did not want to give him time to get away—or to take Wardenford hostage with a weapon. But if he had already made his attack, then time was of the essence. Knocking on the door and shouting their presence seemed to be off the table.

Breaking the door down, then?

Zoe squared her shoulders, thinking about where she would need to kick it for the maximum chance of the wood around the lock splintering and giving way, but Shelley reached out for the door handle and turned it.

It opened.

Another glance exchanged. In unison, Zoe and Shelley drew their guns out of their holsters and held them ready at their sides.

Shelley pushed the door open slowly. It did not creak. They could hear the ringtone louder now. A good distraction which would cover the sound of their footsteps.

For a brief moment, Zoe entertained a fantasy in which Wardenford answered the phone in a drunken stupor, having forgotten to lock the door, and they discovered that he was totally alone.

Then the moment was gone, because she knew it could only be a fantasy.

Together they moved down the hall toward the area where Wardenford had led them before, where the phone was ringing. Zoe took the lead, bringing her firearm up to a more ready position as she approached the junction where everything would become clear. She took a single steadying breath, then sprang forward, pointing her gun into the room.

"Freeze! FBI!" The words came out automatically, a gut reaction to seeing someone standing in the room. Even before her brain had deduced who it was, she knew she had to shout it.

But she didn't need any kind of specialist training to know who was standing in the room. He was five foot nine, one hundred and thirty-nine pounds, and he matched the photograph she had seen on his student ID. More telling than that, he was standing over the prone body of James Wardenford, with a heavy lamp in his hands.

They all froze for a moment, Matthias apparently assessing his options while Zoe took the scene in. Her eyes were drawn to something dark and glittering on the floor—something like dark shards—the shards of a wine bottle, she realized, before the second realization: that she had allowed herself to be distracted too far, her eyes dropping down too low, and she had not seen the telltale bunching of muscles before it was too late.

The only thing that she could do was to catch the lamp that Matthias had thrown at her, before it hit her and knocked her down. She fumbled with her gun, trying desperately not to drop either of them. With the safety off and Wardenford at her feet, both could be catastrophic.

She steadied herself and reversed the momentum to throw the lamp to bounce harmlessly on the sofa cushions, but Matthias was gone—leaping over to the far windows, and then rattling onto the fire escape, his feet making clanging drums of the metal structure.

"Check on him," Zoe shouted to Shelley, who was behind her and unable to make good the pursuit, as she herself launched after Matthias. They couldn't leave an injured and possibly dying victim alone. She dived through the window and onto the fire escape, registering even as she did so that she would now be going after a deadly killer—alone.

Shelley bent swiftly to fit two fingers to James Wardenford's neck, relieved to find a pulse beating there and the warmth of a body. She was even more relieved to hear him groan softly, his eyelids fluttering open and shut as he attempted to fight through the pain and confusion.

His shoulders started to move. Shelley crouched beside him, doing her best to avoid crunching shards of glass and a thin trail of blood that was coming from his head, and placed her hand firmly on top of his back. "Stay still," she said. "Don't try to move. I'll call for help."

Being in law enforcement had one key advantage that Shelley had always loved: the ability to get directly in touch with other life-saving services and get them to someone who needed them as soon as possible. She dialed quickly and relayed the information about where she was and how Wardenford had been injured, then cut the call and focused on soothing him.

Somewhere out there, Zoe was chasing a killer. Shelley strained her ears, listening for any sound outside the window. After their rattling footsteps on the fire escape faded away, there was nothing. No gunshots, which was good.

No sound of any kind that she could identify, over the sound of traffic and people talking and general life in the city, which might be very bad indeed.

She was distracted for too long. Thinking, wondering about Zoe. She was supposed to be paying attention to him. His eyes were closing, and he was going ashy pale.

Shelley swore, kneeling down by Wardenford's head, wincing as an errant piece of glass found its way through her trousers to nick her skin. "Don't do this," she begged, touching his face, shaking his shoulder gently. "Come on, James. Stay with me. The ambulance is nearly here. You just have to stay awake for a few minutes. You can do this."

The sound of a siren in the road outside made Shelley catch her breath. But Wardenford's eyes remained closed, and she could barely detect his breathing.

"No, come on!" she shouted, pinching the skin on his neck to give him a sharp shock and get his attention. "Come on, James. Don't go to sleep. They're here. They're coming to save you. Don't give up!"

Zoe reached inside her lungs for extra breath, reached inside her legs for more power to leap and run faster. It was no use. Matthias was young and fit, and he had a head start. Maybe if he stumbled, fell, got stuck behind a slow-moving pedestrian or hit by a vehicle, she could catch up. It was a long shot maybe.

Where was he going? He was not familiar enough with the neighborhood, surely, to know shortcuts and quick switches—he was moving down roads and between houses at a seemingly random rate, glancing over his shoulder when he made turns to see that she was still there behind him.

She was getting further and further away.

Almost far enough that if he took two turns in quick succession, she wouldn't be able to figure out where he had gone.

No—it couldn't end like this. Zoe couldn't let him get away, out there to potentially harm someone else or to even end up disappearing forever. The kid might have had neurological problems, but underneath that he was still smart. Unfortunately, thanks to the growing need for kids at good schools to have extracurricular activities under their belt in order to compete with the other perfect grades, he was also fast.

He'd been given a perfect bill of health in his medical report, except for that TBI.

Dammit! Zoe cursed as she stumbled on a loose paving slab. This part of the city was not as well-maintained as the areas she was used to, apartment blocks with overgrown yards and weeds springing up to disrupt the pavement. The roads were wide, telegraph poles leaning at odd angles where cars had hit their bases and papered-over cracks in the tarmac, but they were also interrupted by tress planted along their edges in happier times. Cars, trees, garbage spilling out of homes, abandoned furniture—it made for a mismatched and staccato pattern that dashed the advantage her abilities gave her, in the way that only human-made chaos could.

"FBI! Stop!" Zoe shouted, then decided it was better to save her breath in the future. There was no way that he was going to stop just because she told him to, and with the way he tore from one side of the sidewalk to the other, crossing empty road, there was no chance of keeping him in her sights for long enough to fire.

Then there was the fact that she was still in a bit of trouble for shooting at an unarmed suspect in their last case, who turned out to be innocent. She couldn't risk making that mistake again. For all she knew, this could turn out to be a comedy of errors in which a concerned neighbor stepped through and lifted a lamp that had been used to bludgeon Wardenford already.

That wasn't it. Matthias was the killer. But Zoe knew she couldn't dare stop running to risk getting off a shot.

There was barely anyone around at this time; those going to work had gone, those staying at home were staying in. A few elderly residents sitting on porches or out front of dilapidated single-family homes stared at her with narrowed eyes as she flew by, but Zoe couldn't spare the time to yell to them or take them in. They couldn't help her. With no way of knowing if he had a hidden knife or a hammer for bludgeoning, she could hardly ask a civilian to tackle him, either.

But Matthias had made a mistake. A set of cast-iron gates up ahead were closed, the only conclusion to the road they were on. He cast a wide-eyed look over his shoulder before speeding up toward them and then vaulting, one hand on the brick posts holding the gates in place as his body flew through the air above them.

Zoe cursed again, this time only in her head to save oxygen. The gates were five feet tall, easy enough for him to get over. She hadn't tried her vaulting skills in a while. This could be a costly delay.

But, there! A footpath to the side with a gate swinging open in the breeze, only a moment's diversion. Zoe took it, reading the sign with a glance as she sped through: it was a cemetery.

That should have sent a shiver up her spine, but instead it sent a thrill.

A cemetery was wide, open-plan. Paths were laid out but could be ignored.

A cemetery had patterns.

She had him now.

Zoe couldn't afford to stop or slow down, but she caught a glimpse of the map as she ran past and then tried to examine it in her mind. She had just enough of an outline—just enough to know how the cemetery was laid out, paths squirming through graves like the branches of a tree.

And over to the left, the church.

Zoe thought quickly. At his current speed, he was outpacing her to the extent that he would be out of the graveyard before she caught up with him. Sticking on the current route, of chasing straight after him, was not a viable option.

Just like back at the campus, she was going to have to find a way to cut him off.

He was looking back over his shoulder every minute or so, continuing to find new bursts of speed every time that he saw she was still in pursuit. How he was doing it, she had no idea. Her own legs were beginning to tire, and she wasn't sure how much she had left in the tank.

She was going to have to take a risk.

She was going to have to give it everything she had.

Chapter Twenty Nine

Now that they were both among the eerily tranquil atmosphere of the grave sites, Zoe knew that her timing was going to be the most important thing. The road path curved slightly ahead, and Matthias was running straight down the path. It was as though, even though he had so far proven himself to be an able and ruthless killer, he still felt squeamish about running over the homes of the dead.

Zoe had no such problem. The dead were dead and gone. They couldn't feel her shoes disturbing their peace.

She waited, waited, wanting to time it perfectly. The window of opportunity was closing. He had to turn, had to turn now and—

Yes! There! He turned to check that she was following, and then looked ahead again. She had time now, maybe thirty seconds that she could guarantee before he would look for her. She darted to the left, just managing to make it down a crooked path that followed the side of the old church building, yanking off her jacket and throwing it over a slanted gravestone by the path as she went.

It was a small enough church, and that was the good news. If it had been some kind of gothic monster, sprawling and gigantic, she would have never made it in time. But it must have been built in a time when the church was short on funding, or else the community itself was still much smaller, and there was no need for a grand building.

She forced her feet to move faster along the twisted paving slabs, right along the side of the church and then a sharp right turn to cross the back of it. She was counting the seconds in her head, imagining him. Thirty-one, thirty-two, thirty-three, thirty-four, thirty-five—*now* she pictured him, swinging his head around to look. Not seeing her. Stumbling, faltering. Scanning the horizon, the paths off to the side. Confused. Seeing the jacket. Wondering if she had fallen. Squinting his eyes to try to make out if that was a body, or just a jacket.

Slow.

Zoe put all her faith and her belief into this one moment. It was a bitter irony to call on faith in a churchyard when she had never believed in God—not the kind of God that could abandon a small child with a mother like hers—but it was not that kind of faith she drew on.

This faith was in herself.

The final push had to be as she came around this next corner, swung around to the right again to bring herself back into full view of the graveyard. The meandering path that Matthias had chosen swung close to the church right at the exact moment that her path emerged from it, and this was her only chance. If she missed him now, it was over. She knew it. The burning in her lungs knew it. The strain in her calves knew it.

Zoe turned the corner, and he was gone.

She had been right in her calculations, both in the distance required and the pattern of his behavior. The speed he put on when he saw her had been matched by the speed that he lost when he could no longer see her. Out in the middle of the path, back there, the church would not have seemed like a threat. It was far away. Disconnected from the red herring clue she had left behind for him.

So where was he?

Zoe stopped dead, her momentum dissipating. She knew she had been right. From here, she could see across the graveyard and the paths they had followed. He was not there. He hadn't gone back.

So, where?

She scanned the headstones, trying to think. There was only a certain radius of distance where he could be, where he could have gone while she was out of sight. Narrow the field down to that. Focus.

He was hiding—he had to be. He had worked out her gambit and tried to use it against her. He was moving slower, must have come almost to a stop when he realized. That narrowed it down more. *Think, Zoe. Where?*

Some of the grave markers were thin—crosses or single slabs of stone. Nothing to hide behind. There were three larger structures within the field of her view. Could he be lying down directly behind them?

None of this made sense. Not really. Why stop like that…?

Unless he was expecting her to run past and carry on, bypassing him completely. If he wanted to use the time to get away, he would have run back the way they came, leaving her scrambling to catch up again. He wasn't on the path or in the distance. He must have thought he would have an advantage of some kind.

There was a rectangular structure not far from the path, coming up on the side. Long but low, an approximation of a coffin in stone. A carving of an angel sat on top of it at the head.

If she was him, if she was determined to fight and end the chase, she would hide there. She would crouch behind the tallest part, the angel, and wait. She could see it playing out in her head. Zoe would run by, somewhat startled, her momentum cut, looking for him. He would wait for her to pass and spring up, perhaps hit her over the head. Knock her out against the stone. Perhaps not stop until she wasn't going to be chasing anyone, ever again.

He meant to kill her.

Zoe's breath caught in her chest, but this was no time to hesitate. No one else was coming—not in enough time that she could rely on their help. If she waited, he might decide to run and get away from her again. She wouldn't be fast enough. They were both still, not yet moving. He would have the advantage from a dead start.

There was only one thing she could do. One path that gave her the potential for a successful outcome.

Zoe didn't think anymore. She crossed the path at a run, rounded the grave marker from the opposite side to where he was expecting her.

He was there! She had no time to think—no time to do anything but react. He was coming for her, a snarl on his face as soon as he saw her. His hands were fists. He meant to do her harm. If she let him, he would knock her down. Only one thing to do—one way to use his momentum against him. Too close to duck or dive—she would have to move—

They connected as she threw herself headlong at him, tackling him to the ground in a mess of limbs and spent breath and hard ground.

Matthias tried to struggle, but Zoe had the advantage of being on top. He managed to get a knee up and aim for her stomach, but she shifted her weight and it slammed into her hip instead. Painful, yes. Not as winding as the stomach would have been.

His leg was between them, enough to give him leverage. If he used it, he could push her, fling her against the stone grave marker. Follow up with a smash to her head. His eyes flicked to the side and she knew he was going to do it.

She rolled.

He yelped in surprise as her momentum drew him over too, first on top and then over again, Zoe's legs grappling for purchase, pushing his down. She flung him to the side with all of her weight so that he was lying on his stomach. She had only a split second before he might get his legs under him. She threw her body forward, covering his, knocking him flat to the ground.

She pulled the handcuffs out from her belt and groped for one of his wrists, fitting them on as he kicked and swore. The second one was even easier.

Just like that, he was done.

He knew it, too. He stopped fighting and lay still. The wind was knocked out of him, and he pressed his face down against the cold floor.

"Matthias Kranz," Zoe panted, feeling the pain as acid flooded her muscles. "I am . . . arresting you . . . for the murder of . . . Ralph Henderson, Cole Davidson . . . and Dr. Edwin North."

The rest of the Miranda warning could wait until they had him in for questioning. For now, Zoe needed every last drop of oxygen in her lungs to call her partner and request backup.

Chapter Thirty

Zoe hung back awkwardly. She was not sure what she should do, now that the moment was here. Inside, she was ecstatic, but that happiness was tempered by the still-guilty knowledge that she had caused all of this in the first place.

Dr. Applewhite stepped out into the reception area, where family members and friends would wait to pick up their loved ones upon their release from custody. Zoe wasn't sure exactly which category she fit into at that moment, but relief flooded her heart when Dr. Applewhite saw her and broke into a smile.

"Zoe! You did it!"

Zoe wasn't often one to give in to physical shows of affection, but for this once, she couldn't help herself. She stepped forward and allowed herself to be embraced by Dr. Applewhite, craving the forgiveness and warmth that came from her arms. As she rested her head over Dr. Applewhite's shoulder, if there were tears that sprang to her eyes, she told herself that it was a result of extreme fatigue and nothing else.

"They told me you caught the actual killer. That's why I'm being released," Dr. Applewhite said, pulling back altogether too early for Zoe's tastes and looking into her face.

Zoe hastily wiped a hand over her eyes. "Early this morning. I came straight to see you as soon as we had him booked. Shelley is preparing to interview hm now."

Dr. Applewhite frowned. "Is it a good idea for you to take part in that? You look exhausted. If your partner has been up all night as well, I'm sure she's feeling the same way."

Zoe gave her a wan smile. "We are FBI agents. If we cannot deal with one night without sleep, we are not worthy of the badge. Besides, this is our case. Handing it off to someone else now would be excruciating."

Dr. Applewhite smiled back ruefully. "Well, I suppose that's the way you do things around here."

"Oh, not at all. If our superior knew, we would be in trouble. Probably sent home to rest."

Dr. Applewhite laughed, and though there was certainly some tiredness in it, at least she could still laugh. "I'd better call my husband, get him to come and get me."

"I already called. I had your home number saved." Zoe nodded toward the parking lot. "I imagine he will be along very soon."

"Thank you, dear." Dr. Applewhite squeezed Zoe's upper arm. "Really. You don't have to wait with me. I know you must be eager to get back to it."

"I do not mind," Zoe said, but then Dr. Applewhite was exclaiming and waving at someone through the door, and her husband was parking the car, and Zoe was no longer needed.

Zoe sat down next to Shelley, sipping at the fresh, hot coffee she had just retrieved from the machine out in the hall. It was so hot it burned, but she needed it. The energy boost would get her through this last little bit of what needed to be done.

According to Shelley, it wouldn't be needed for long. Before they entered, they had observed Matthias through the one-way mirror, and Shelley was confident that he would talk. Zoe settled into her chair, uncomfortable as it was, looking forward to watching Shelley do what she did best.

"So, Mr. Kranz," Shelley said, pretending to consult her notes. An old trick. As if she hadn't already memorized everything on the pages. "Why don't we start right at the beginning—with your accident?"

Matthias Kranz was surly, arms folded across his chest, gaze fixed firmly on the table. Even so, there was something curiously blank and detached about his expression as he spoke.

"Huh. Accident. Funny."

"What do you mean by that?"

Matthias looked up, his eyes spitting venom as they fixed on Shelley. Even Zoe could see the hate radiating from them. "Hell of a coincidence. You ask me, not an accident at all. A—a—push."

"A push?"

Matthias snarled. "Don't jo—jo—mock me."

Shelley raised her chin an inch, something clearing up in her eyes. Zoe watched her with amazement. She wasn't quite sure about what was going on, but watching Shelley read everything she needed to know from tone and body language was like a master class.

Zoe wondered briefly if this was what it was like for Shelley, to watch Zoe work with numbers.

"You mean, you think it was a set-up?" Shelley said, with new understanding. "Someone made you crash your car."

"Something was tampered with. The brakes or something. No way it was me that crashed like that. I'm better at driving my—my..."

"Your car."

"Yes!"

Shelley nodded and made some quick notes in pen on the sheet that she was looking at. Zoe read over her shoulder: *delusional.*

"All right. And what was their motive, whoever did this?"

"They knew," Matthias said, sneering and jabbing a finger toward his own head. "They knew."

Shelley's eyes narrowed momentarily before she spoke again. Watching her, Zoe understood intuitively that she was reading, interpreting. That she was waiting for the pattern to clear up in her head, the way that Zoe would stare at a complex equation or series of numbers and wait for them to make sense in the context of the case.

"You believe that someone targeted you because of your gift with mathematics?" Shelley asked.

Matthias nodded vigorously. Perhaps he did not trust himself to get the right words.

"Okay. And after the accident, what changed?" Shelley's agreement was light, uncomplicated. Not exactly a statement that she believed him, but not a judgment either. Something that could be taken as reassurance for a person who needed to hear it.

"Everything. The, um. The, um. The—the snakes."

"Snakes?"

Matthias gestured toward his head again, bowing his neck, his gaze back to the table. "The snakes. I can't—get there."

There was a pause while Shelley watched him. "There's something wrong in your head now, isn't there, Matthias?"

He slammed a hand down on the table with loud and sudden force, enough to make Zoe—in her tired state—jump. His voice was strained when he spoke, and she was more than a little surprised to see tears escaping down his cheeks. "Everything's wrong. Everything I had—all I worked for—the snakes ate it all up."

"Talk us through what happened, in your own words."

"There was a—a—a paper. Physics with the new guy. Professor Wardenford was gone. Cole was the SI. I—didn't—I f—I…"

"You failed the paper." Shelley was leaning forward in her seat, paying close attention. There was some kind of synergy between them now, some kind of wavelength that was working. She was understanding him.

"Yes." Matthias hung his head. "I got my words mixed up. Had to explain a—known theory and I got my words mixed up. Then the numbers. He told the other one. Professor Henderson."

"So, Cole Davidson was the first person who noticed you were having difficulties. That was why you killed him?"

Matthias's eyes had hardened like flint. "Henderson, he had me take these—exams. Not exams, but…"

"Tests," Shelley supplied.

"Tests. He came back and said I probably had dyslexia. But the numbers were off too and he thought that was strange. Then he told—then he told *Cole*."

"Did Cole bring it up in class?"

"He offered *help*. Said I might need more—hours for my work. Get extra time on my deadlines."

"What happened next?" Shelley leaned her head on steepled fingers, listening carefully.

"Sent me to Dr. North." Matthias's anger flared up again, and he kicked the metal table legs to either side of him. "Snakes—saw the snakes. He found the snakes all knotted up and he showed me. Showed me how I was changed."

The picture was emerging. Every single victim, someone who had simply known about Matthias's problems. Someone who had been instrumental in diagnosing them. Even though the injury was not the fault of any one of them, Matthias had latched his anger—which had no other outlet—onto them. One by one.

"The doctor was one of the people who tried to help you. Why kill him?"

Matthias scoffed, his hands bunched into tight fists on the table. "Help me? He said the snakes were—were there to stay. No way to kill them. Just have to live with them. Take pill this or pill that, make it better. Happy snakes. But always still the snakes."

Shelley moved down her notes, to the final line. "What about your Professor Wardenford? We've heard that you looked up to him, even considered him a mentor. Why did you go to kill him?"

"He didn't know." There was real regret in Matthias's eyes, at least as far as Zoe knew what it looked like in order to diagnose it. Another tear slipped down his cheek. His emotions were swinging wildly out of control. "I just wanted to talk. He didn't know about the snakes like everyone else did. But then he knew. I saw it. I told him the time and I knew the snakes spat it out all wrong."

"So you attacked him as well." There was a little reproach in Shelley's voice, creeping in as if she couldn't help it.

"Is he . . . ?"

Shelley met his eyes directly, eschewing a smile. "James Wardenford is in the hospital being treated for a fractured skull. They say he will pull through just fine."

Matthias sighed, another flood of tears escaping from his eyes.

"There's one thing I don't yet understand," Shelley said, flicking to another page of her notes. Here was a blown-up image of each of the equations, along with Dr. Applewhite's theoretical calculations below. "You deliberately implicated Dr. Francesca Applewhite. You planted her hairs at Dr. North's home, am I correct?"

He nodded.

"For the tape," Zoe said, quietly, "the suspect nodded." She wanted to make sure the records were absolutely clear on that part.

"You must have had to do some very creative work to get hold of those hairs, and to place them so carefully," Shelley continued.

Matthias smiled faintly at the praise. "Got from her office chair. People's head—head—hair falls out. They just leave it there. Easy to take."

"What I don't understand is why it had to be her. This was a focused decision, but as far as I can see, Dr. Applewhite has no involvement in your medical history. She hadn't even met you."

Matthias scoffed, his facing turning into a mask of disgust. "I didn't need to meet her. She went and published that faulty equation for everyone to see, hasn't she? She will ask for help from others. Couldn't even get it right herself."

Zoe's head hurt. It was hard enough keeping up with the way normal people spoke. Matthias was a nightmare—tenses changing, words out of order, misused. She was thinking that she would probably have to ask Shelley for a full translation once this was over. Matthias clearly tried to talk as little as possible to hide his defects, but he could not help himself—he wasn't yet used to staying quiet. He had to explain himself.

"So, this was about the equation—the one that you included in your own equations?" Shelley prompted.

"You figured it out, huh? Well, I'm impressed." Matthias leaned back in his chair, looking off to the side as he thought. "Mind you, you did have Professor Wardenford's help. But anyway, I solved it. I—found it. I had it all ready, just needed to write something up so that I could publish it. In a real journal. My first one."

Zoe noticed that he seemed to be clearer when he talked about the things he cared about the most. It was as if the anger was driving his focus, allowing him to get closer to the issue, find the right words.

"That must have been disappointing."

Zoe almost missed it—Shelley's words came out of left field for her. Disappointing, how? But she looked at Mattias and how he seemed to agree in every line of his downcast posture and expression, and it dawned on her. Ah. He couldn't publish a paper if he couldn't write one. Not only that, but even if he managed it, his debut publication would be his last. His bright future, extinguished in a single crash.

"I wanted that—dog to know. I wanted her to know someone else had solved it. I wanted her to know that I was smarter than her. And then I wanted her to pay for publishing something like that without getting it right. I knew you'd let—Teacher Wardenford go if you thought it was her."

"You included yourself in the equation too, didn't you?"

He looked up, almost with shock. "You saw that?"

"The capital 'M.' It was hard to miss."

He looked down at the table, his eyes moving over invisible patterns there. Trapped by his own hubris. His need to leave a signature. Perhaps he had never imagined that law enforcement would be smart enough to spot it.

They were almost done. All of the loose ends were tied up: they had his motivation, his method, and his confessions. There would be time later, after they'd all had a good sleep, to go back in exhaustive detail and find out how he committed each crime in the minutiae. It was unlikely that he would try to protest his innocence in court, and even if he did, the evidence they had against him was building. They had access to credit card records now, to his phone records, to his license plate that could be traced through surveillance footage to track his movements. They had him up against the wall, and he knew it.

But Zoe wanted to clear up one last thing, before she let him go and sit in a cell for a few hours.

"I have the report from your car accident here, Mr. Kranz," she said.

That got his attention. He looked up at her, eyes narrowed slightly, waiting to see what she would say.

"The interesting thing," Zoe continued, "is that there was an investigation into the accident, because at first it was not clear what had happened. You claimed no memory of the events, and it was important to find out whether the car was faulty and so on. Well, it says here that they figured out what had happened after looking into your cell phone records. You were in the middle of a text conversation at the moment of the accident. In fact, you had just fired off a message when you lost control of the car."

"Lies," Matthias hissed. He made to lunge at her, or perhaps at the report, but all he accomplished was to rattle the chains of his handcuffs against the desk.

"We will be seeing you later, Mr. Kranz," Zoe promised, standing up. "For now, this interview is terminated."

She exchanged a look with Shelley, and they left the room, walking away from the seething rage and indecipherable noises that were issuing from Matthias Kranz.

Chapter Thirty One

"That is the last of it." Zoe placed one more piece of paper on top of the pile they had worked through together. "Everything should be in place now."

"I hope you're right about this idea of doing all the paperwork first so you can relax later," Shelley said. "I don't know about you, but I'm exhausted. I could sleep for a week. I probably made a ton of mistakes."

"You did not. I was checking," Zoe said, gathering the neat pile and pushing it into a folder for easier filing. "I will get these over to SAIC Maitland. You can go home."

"Are you sure?" Shelley asked. "Wait—Zoe, didn't you get a lift here? Where's your car?"

Zoe had to think about it for an embarrassingly long time, tracing back all of her steps across the morning, the night, and the evening before. "I left it at home. I got the subway to meet John, and he drove me here."

"I'll wait and drop you home first, then," Shelley said.

"You do not have to do that. I am capable of getting home by myself."

"I know you are. But as your partner, I'd like to make that easier for you." Shelley paused and ran a hand back over her hair, checking whether it was still neatly fitted into her ponytail. It was. "Zoe, I… I wanted to apologize. I think sometimes I think of you as being this fragile person that needs protecting from the outside world, but that's not it at all. You know what's good for you. I just have to listen to what you're telling me, and stop going all Mama Bear about making sure you eat and sleep and relax."

Zoe paused, considering what her partner had said. It was true, she had noticed that mothering instinct in Shelley. It had caused problems, too. But there was more to it than that. "I appreciate that you care," she admitted. "I know you mean well. I suppose I am trying to please you in my own way, too. It is just that I am not like other people. I cannot do all of the things that other people can."

"I know that now. Forcing you into social situations—even if I don't think of them as social, like my home—I won't do that again."

Zoe sighed. She sat back down in her chair, realizing that this was more than just a quick chat. "That was my fault. I wanted to have dinner with your family. In other circumstances, it might have been good."

"So, what was it?" Shelley asked, sitting next to her again.

"With Dr. Applewhite . . . I felt that I had done a great wrong. I have no one else, just her. And when I saw your perfect, beautiful family—your life—everything that you have, I . . ." Zoe took a deep breath before admitting t out loud. "I got jealous."

"You don't need to be jealous of me," Shelley half-laughed. "I mean, god, my life isn't perfect. Amelia is a kid like any other. She pees the bed sometimes and drops food all over the floor and draws on the walls. And me and Harry, we argue. All the time, about silly little things."

"At least you have a husband and a child," Zoe pointed out. "But it does not matter. I know now. I do not need to be jealous of you anymore."

"Because you know it's not perfect?"

Zoe shook her head. "Because I can have that for myself. I can work hard and strive for the life that I want." She took a breath again, realizing that what she was about to say was true. "The life I now finally know that I deserve."

Shelley squeezed Zoe's hand silently, a gesture of support and togetherness. There was peace for a moment, neither of them stirring or saying a word.

"Damn," Zoe said then, getting up from her chair to resume where they had left off. "I guess that therapist I have been seeing is pretty good, after all."

Epilogue

Zoe settled down opposite Dr. Monk. She had never really appreciated before how comfortable the chairs in her therapy room were. The leather armchair was perfectly worn and used, not yet to the point of losing the softness of its cushions and yet molded into the right shape for a human body.

Just like Dr. Monk itself, it had learned how to embrace each of the patients who came in and sat down, and make them feel right at home.

"I'll be with you in one moment," Dr. Monk said, from her desk at the other end of the room. "I'll just finish this memo and then we can begin our session."

Zoe dug her cell out of her pocket, thinking that now was a good time to set it on silent. Then she hesitated, looking at the screen.

It could be a good time to do something else, too.

Before she could lose her nerve, she wrote up a new message and sent it, only reading it over once to check for errors. Not the dozens of times she might otherwise have wasted, proofreading and redrafting to try to make it sound more like something a normal person would say.

Are you free this Saturday? I'd love to go on our next date.

There was only a brief pause before John sent a message in response.

YES! 7pm? I'll pick you up?

Zoe smiled to herself. She could do a whole lot worse than John. And, for the first time in a long time, she did not add an old habitual thought: that he could do so much better than her.

"All right, I'm sorry to keep you waiting," Dr. Monk said, sitting opposite Zoe and shuffling the pages of her notebook to find the right session. "How are we doing today, then?"

Zoe cleared her throat and looked up to meet her therapist's eyes. "Actually, Dr. Monk, I have something to tell you," she said.

"Is it something to do with that message you just received that had you lighting up like a Christmas tree?" Dr. Monk smiled conspiratorially.

"No," Zoe said. "Well, yes. I will tell you about that later. But there is something else first."

"I'm listening." Dr. Monk nodded.

Zoe took a deep breath. It was time. There was no more putting it off now. "I have synesthesia," she said. "I see numbers everywhere. I understand them intuitively. It's how I'm able to solve many of our cases. It's a special ability I have."

Dr. Monk nodded again, her pen poised above the page. There was no flicker of revulsion across her face. There was no recoiling in horror. In fact, she barely gave any sign of a reaction at all, as if what Zoe had told her was perfectly normal. "I see. Can you tell me more about that?"

And Zoe did—and, for something that she had feared for such a long time, it turned out to be not so awful at all.

Now Available for Pre-Order!

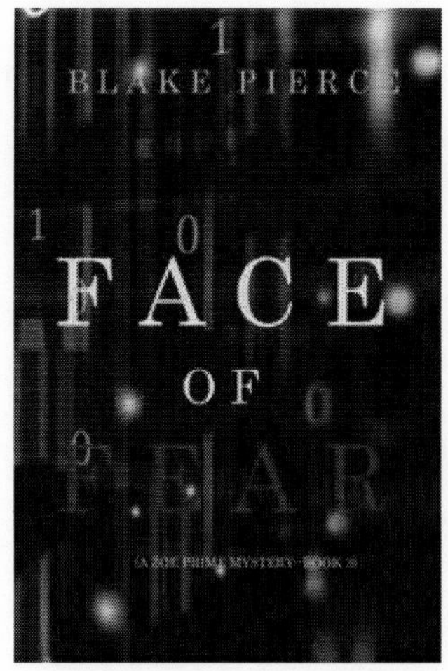

FACE OF FEAR
(A Zoe Prime Mystery—Book 3)

"A MASTERPIECE OF THRILLER AND MYSTERY. Blake Pierce did a magnificent job developing characters with a psychological side so well described that we feel inside their minds, follow their fears and cheer for their success. Full of twists, this book will keep you awake until the turn of the last page."

—Books and Movie Reviews, Roberto Mattos (re Once Gone)

FACE OF FEAR is book #3 in a new FBI thriller series by USA Today bestselling author Blake Pierce, whose #1 bestseller Once Gone (Book #1) (a free download) has received over 1,000 five star reviews.

FBI Special Agent Zoe Prime suffers from a rare condition which also gives her a unique talent—she views the world through a lens of numbers. The numbers torment her, make her unable to relate to people, and give her a failed romantic life—yet they also allow her to see patterns that no other FBI agent can see. Zoe keeps her condition a secret, ashamed, in fear her colleagues may find out.

Women are turning up dead in Los Angeles, with no pattern other than the fact that they are all heavily tattooed. With a dead end in the case, the FBI calls in Special Agent Zoe prime to find a pattern where others cannot–and to stop the killer before he strikes again.

But Zoe, in therapy, is battling her own demons, barely able to function in her world plagued by numbers and on the brink of quitting the FBI. Can she really enter this psychotic killer's mind, find the hidden pattern, and come out unscathed?

An action-packed thriller with heart-pounding suspense, FACE OF FEAR is book #3 in a riveting new series that will leave you turning pages late into the night.

Book #4 will be available soon.

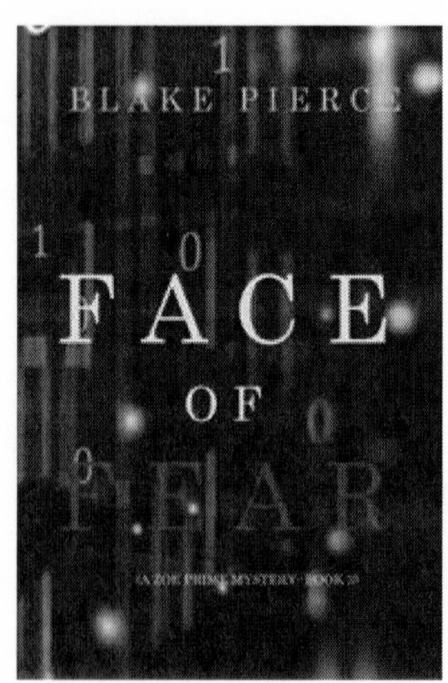

FACE OF FEAR
(A Zoe Prime Mystery–Book 3)

Made in United States
North Haven, CT
27 November 2022